And

The Ring

The Cross And The Ring

Richard Miskin

Marshall Pickering

For Jane and John

Pickering and Inglis
Marshall Pickering
3 Beggarwood Lane, Basingstoke, Hants RG23 7LP, UK

Copyright © 1986 by Richard Miskin
First published in 1986 by Pickering and Inglis Ltd
Part of the Marshall Pickering Holdings Group
A subsidiary of the Zondervan Corporation

All rights reserved. No part of this publication may be reproduced, stored in a retrieval system, or transmitted, in any form or by any means, electronic, mechanical, photocopying, recording or otherwise, without the prior permission in writing, of the publisher

British Library CIP Data

Miskin, Richard
  The cross and the ring.
  I. Title
  823'.914[J] PZ7

ISBN 0-7208-2374-9

Text set in Plantin by
Brian Robinson, Buckingham
Printed in Great Britain by
Anchor Brendon Ltd., Tiptree, Essex.

Chapter One

As soon as the children had fallen asleep in their warm beds, the cold, white snow began to fall. It floated lazily down hour after hour while they slept. It fell on the roofs of the houses, turning them into white, steep mountains, and on the roads which became frozen white rivers. And it fell silently on the huge old tree in the garden, gradually weighing it down with a covering of snow that was the heaviest load it had ever had to support. A load that was to force it to give up the secrets it had hidden for so long.

Although anyone could see that the tree was very old, it was the snow that fell on this night before Christmas that finally forced it to reveal its secrets, and it was these secrets which carried Simon and Sandy back into a time long past in a distant and warmer land. Yet, strangely, it was a land they had both known before, a land where they felt they belonged, and where Sandy felt as much a part of it as she did now in her narrow bed at the top of the house when the first light of day peeped through the curtains.

She stretched and yawned, pulled the duvet over her head and tried to go to sleep again. But it was no good. Something was different. She sat up suddenly, and then she knew what it was. The room felt colder than she had ever known it. Then she remembered that it was nearly Christmas, and running to the window she gave a squeal of delight as she saw the whole garden covered with a thick blanket of snow.

It was so beautiful that it made her gasp. She closed her eyes tight, and then opened them again to make sure it was all still there. It was.

'I shall remember this moment as long as I live,' she whispered to herself.

She shut the window, put on her dressing gown and hurried through the open door which separated her room from her brother Simon's.

Simon was fast asleep. He was twelve years old: two years older than Sandy. They both went to the same school, and most of the time, though not always, they liked to play the same games. They always seemed to be together, and people said how nice – and unusual – it was to see a sister and brother so fond of each other.

Sandy shook her brother gently to wake him up. He turned over towards her and opened his eyes.

'Come and see,' she said.

'See what?' he replied sleepily. 'It's much too early to look at anything. Do go back to bed.' He was turning over and was just about to put his head under the pillow when he heard Sandy say one word.

'Snow!'

He threw off the duvet, jumped out of bed and they both ran together back to Sandy's room and stood looking out at the garden below.

'Wow!' said Simon softly as they gazed at the white world outside. 'It's just like a picture book. Like magic. Fantastic!'

The branches of the trees in the garden were bowed down with the weight of the snow that they carried. One very old elm tree on the far side of the lawn that their father always called 'Old Dutch' was leaning across towards them carrying so much snow that it looked as if it would topple over any moment onto the house.

Downstairs in the kitchen their father was having his breakfast. He was a doctor. His wife, the children's mother, had died when the children were too small to remember. He loved his children more than anything else in the world. He knew how much they depended on him and how much they loved him. His work as a doctor kept him busy in his consulting-rooms in the town for most of the day and often he was called out at night. This worried him as the children were left to fend for themselves, until, one day an old school friend of his wife had come to stay for the weekend, and she had been there ever since.

Miss Bell (everyone called her 'Ding) was cook, housekeeper, mother to the children and friend to all who knew her. The children adored her. She was the same age as the doctor, and full of fun. But she had strict standards of behaviour, and when their father tended to spoil them she could (and often did) say *'No!'* They respected her for it and their father supported her. This was one of the reasons that they were such a happy family.

'The children are very quiet,' said the doctor, helping himself to another piece of toast. He sighed and smiled at Ding.

'That means they are doing something they shouldn't be doing.'

Ding put a cup of coffee before him and returned to the stove where she was frying some eggs for the children.

'I expect they'll want to go out and play in the snow,' she said.

'Not before they've had their breakfast,' said the doctor. 'I'll go and see.'

They heard the door open and turned as he came in. He walked over to the window and stood behind them with his hands on their shoulders, looking out over the sea of white.

Suddenly from somewhere out in the garden they heard a loud crack. The noise broke the stillness like a rifle shot.

'It's Old Dutch,' said Simon. 'Look, he's moving!' Sandy noticed that the very top branches were swaying from side to side, and now they saw that one of the huge dead branches was falling. Then, slowly the tree began to fall towards them.

'The whole tree's coming down!' shouted their father. 'I think it's going to fall on the house!' He looked round. 'Quick! Under the bed!'

They all dived for Sandy's bed, but it was a box-bed and there wasn't room to get underneath, and as they all lay on the floor not knowing quite what to do, Simon began to giggle, and Sandy closed her eyes expecting the tree to crash through the roof on top of them.

It seemed a long time coming. Then suddenly there was a long drawn-out groan, another crack and a longer rending and splintering kind of sound. Then a very loud bump, and all was quiet.

They all got up and rushed to the window.

Old Dutch lay right across the lawn from one end to the other. What was left of the top branch had missed the house by only a few feet. Most of the snow that had lain so thickly on the boughs and branches had fallen off. Everything, except the thick trunk, looked twisted and bent and where the great tree had stood so proudly at the end of the lawn for so many years there was now a gaping round hole. Not only had most of the roots come away with the tree, but a huge round mass of soil still stuck to them, making the base of the fallen tree look like a huge round plum-pudding.

'Poor Old Dutch,' sighed Dad. 'I shall have to get someone to saw him up and cart him away. What a sad end. I used to have tea under his branches when I was a small boy, and my father and his father also. But it went back farther than that. I remember my father telling me that Old Dutch was planted there to mark the site of a grave or something.'

Looking at his watch, he made his way to the door. 'And if you're not downstairs in exactly seven minutes I shall . . . I shall . . . ' He could never think of a punishment for them and they loved him for it. They ran over to him and gave him their usual 'good morning' kisses and hugs.

'You have only a few minutes left,' he laughed, pretending to look at his watch again, 'and the last one down cleans the car this evening.'

'But, Dad, we'd freeze to death!' said Sandy, opening her eyes wide and pretending to be frightened.

'Three minutes only,' replied Dad, and as they rushed to wash and get dressed, he returned to the kitchen to finish his breakfast.

'Simon!' shouted Sandy through the open door joining their rooms. 'We *must* go and see Old Dutch.

We can have a snowball fight as well.'

'All right,' replied Simon, 'we'll go down the back stairs for woollies and wellies, out the side door, and be back for breakfast before Ding notices.'

They were soon in the garden enjoying the crunch of the snow under their feet as they ran together to see the tree and the hole it had left.

'Heck!' said Simon, as they reached the edge and looked down the hole. 'It's jolly deep.'

It was not only deep, but wide as well.

Simon scrambled down into the hole, fell over and rolled to the bottom.

'Look!' he shouted, as he picked himself up. 'There are some old bits of leather. It looks like an old bag. And look,' he shouted in excitement again, pulling out something from the earth at the side of the hole. 'It's a little cross!'

But Sandy was not looking. At least she was not looking at Simon. She was looking at the huge mound of earth and roots on the other side. In the centre, mixed up with the dark soil something was sparkling. It was very small, but it was so bright that she had to half-close her eyes for a second.

For a reason that she couldn't explain, she suddenly felt very excited. It was as if the little shining object was trying to tell her something.

She opened her mouth to tell Simon, but at that moment Ding called to them through the kitchen window to come in and have their breakfast.

Chapter Two

It always seemed to happen, thought Sandy, that when they were doing something exciting outside in the garden like climbing a tree or watching a bird's nest, they were called inside.

'Oh no!' wailed Simon, 'I've just found something interesting and we have to go.'

'Simon,' said Sandy, 'can you see what's shining up there in the earth near that twisted root?'

He looked up from the bottom of the hole. 'I can't see anything shining,' he said.

Sandy walked round the edge of the hole to where the huge mass of roots and soil lay. It was much higher than she was and she couldn't reach round because of the hole. The only way to reach it, she thought, was with a ladder propped up in the hole against the roots. She decided to bring one from the toolshed after breakfast.

Simon climbed out of the hole. 'I'll race you to the kitchen!' he shouted. He won the race (as he usually did), and they were soon eating their breakfast in the warm kitchen.

Dad had already left for his surgery in the town and Ding had been a little angry with them for slipping outside before breakfast.

Simon, having finished his breakfast, pulled the little cross from his pocket and put it on the table. It was smaller than his little finger. It looked as if it were made of iron, but there was no rust to be seen.

Ding picked it up and looked at it, then took it and washed it under the tap at the sink. She brought it back and put it on the table. Now that it was clean the first thing they noticed was a small hole that had been made in the top. Also the corners were now bright and shining.

'It looks very old,' said Ding, 'and I think the hole must be for wire or string to go through for it to hang round the neck. She sat down beside them and held it again in the palm of her hand. 'It's very heavy for its size,' she said. Then she turned to the children with a look of complete surprise. 'I do believe it's solid gold!' she said with excitement. 'Simon, bring the metal polish and the duster from the drawer quickly!'

They soon had it gleaming and bright, and now

that it was clean and polished they noticed that on one side of the upright there was a clear engraving of a fish.

'That's a funny thing to have on a cross,' said Ding. 'It's the secret sign of the early Christians, but I've never seen one on a cross before. And I'm quite sure that it's gold. You must take great care of it, Simon.'

She got up, went to the drawer and took out a piece of string. Threading one end through the little hole on the top of the cross, she tied the ends and handed it to Simon. He put it over his head and it hung around his neck in the 'v' of his shirt. It felt warm against his skin, and comfortable, as if it had been specially made for him.

Now they were all very excited and Sandy was impatient to get back to the tree to see what her shining thing was. They both hurried through the last of their breakfast and at last they were ready to return.

Ding, on hearing about Sandy's find and also that she was going to use a ladder, decided to come too. They collected the ladder from the shed and were soon back at the hole. Simon jumped down and Ding and Sandy passed the ladder to him.

'Where's the thing you saw, Sandy?' he asked.

Sandy pointed at the roots and said, 'There it is, can't you see it shining?'

'Sandy!' said Simon impatiently, 'I'm not stupid,

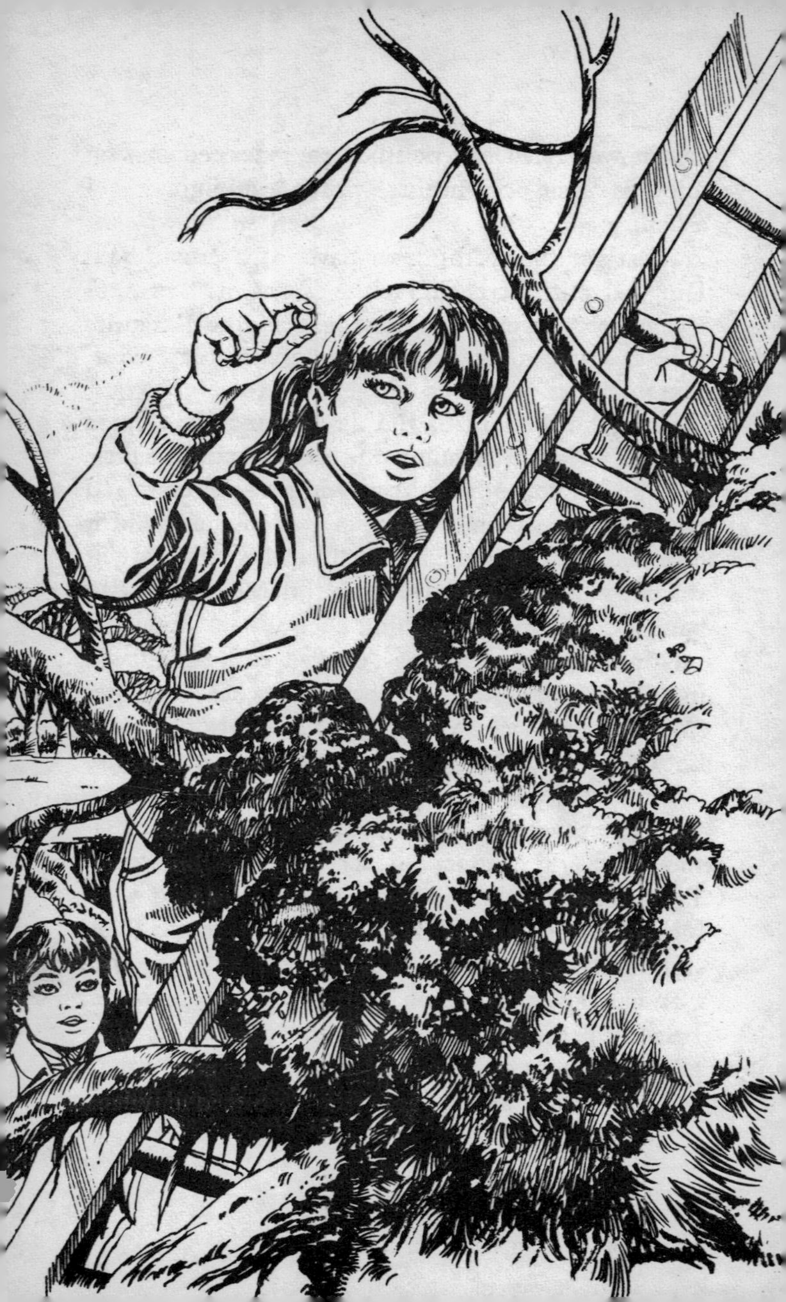

you know.' He looked again at where she was pointing, 'But I can't see anything at all.'

Ding couldn't see anything either, so Sandy slid down and climbed up the ladder which Simon had put up against the roots.

She felt a great excitement as she climbed steadily upwards, Simon holding the bottom of the ladder steady for her. As she got higher, and nearer to the shining object, she felt that all her life she had been waiting for this moment. She put out her right hand, grasped it, and pulled it gently out of the earth. It was a ring! She blew some of the soil off it and looked at it carefully. It needed a good clean but it was made of exactly the same metal as the cross. In one place it had been scratched by a stone or something, and that is what had shone so brightly, just like gold.

'What is it?' shouted Ding, stamping her foot on the snow trying to keep warm.

'Do hurry up, Sandy,' said Simon, using the voice that older brothers always use to younger sisters, 'I can't hold this ladder all day. Have you found anything?'

'Yes,' replied Sandy, looking down at them. She was so excited that she could hardly speak.

'It's a ring, and I think it's made of gold like the cross!'

She couldn't resist the temptation to see if it fitted her finger. She put her arm round the ladder, opened the fingers of her left hand and slipped it onto her forefinger. It was a little tight, so she twisted it gently to ease it on.

Suddenly she felt very giddy. Everything became very dark and her head seemed to be filled with the noise of a terrible storm. A gale-strong wind howled round her trying to tear her off the ladder. Her ears were deafened with the crash of thunder. She was so frightened that she nearly fell off. Then everything became blurred and above the noise of the wind and thunder a voice seemed to be saying 'The cross! The cross!' Then, as suddenly as it had all begun, it all stopped and all was quiet again. No wind. No noise.

She looked down. Simon was still there as if nothing had happened. He still had one hand on the ladder, but in the other he was holding onto the little cross hanging from his neck. He was looking at her in a puzzled sort of way.

'Are you all right?' he asked.

'Yes,' she replied, 'yes I'm all right.'

'You shouted something about the cross,' he said, holding it out for her to see.

At the sight of the little cross Sandy felt much calmer after being so frightened. She was still confused, and she knew that in some way it was all connected with the cross and the ring. She climbed down the ladder and showed them the ring.

'It's the same as the cross,' said Ding. 'And probably made by the same craftsman.'

'I bet it was owned by the same person,' said Simon – 'But how on earth did they get in the roots of the Old Dutch?'

Nobody had an answer. They looked around in the hole for a while to make sure they hadn't missed anything. Then they walked up the length of the fallen tree, looking at the smashed branches, and into the house.

Sandy washed and polished the ring. Not only was it gold, but it had the same fish engraved on it as the cross had. After her fright on the ladder, which she knew had something to do with the ring, she didn't want to wear it again just yet, so she went up to her room and put it under her pillow.

The children decided to telephone their father to tell him of their finds. Luckily he had just seen his last patient for the morning and was resting in his surgery with his feet up on his desk. He wrote some notes of some of the things they told him, and promised to be home as soon as he could.

'Tell him not to forget the Christmas tree,' shouted Ding from the kitchen before they hung up.

He arrived home soon after dark with the tree and many parcels, a huge turkey and some mistletoe for kissing under. He seemed very excited about something, and as soon as they had taken everything out of the car into the house he couldn't wait any longer.

'I too have made an interesting discovery,' he told

them. 'First you must show me yours, and then I'll tell you about mine.'

Sandy dashed upstairs to get her ring, and soon they were all seated round the kitchen table, the doctor examining their finds with interest.

He had, he said, been round to the local museum and library where he had spent some time trying to find out about the history of their own area, especially where the house stood. He had looked into many old books seeking for a clue to explain how the cross and the ring came to be underneath Old Dutch, and this is what he had found out.

'About five hundred years ago,' he said, 'there was a large monastery right where we are now. It was very rich and King Henry the Eighth ordered all the valuable things to be given to him and the monks were to be driven out or killed.'

'One night,' went on the doctor, 'soldiers arrived in the district to carry out his orders. But before they reached the monastery a man on a horse galloped up to the gates and warned them all to run away. They were so frightened that they all ran off into the night, except –' here the doctor paused to light his pipe, smiling at the children's impatience for him to continue – 'except for one young monk.'

The doctor pulled an old and tattered book from his pocket and opened it to where a piece of newspaper had been left to mark the place.

'This book was written by that same young monk

when he was much older, and right in the middle here he described exactly what he did on that night.

'When all the monks had fled, I went straightway to the Chapel to save the cross and the ring. They had been brought to England by a Christian from Rome in the year of our Lord 1227, and were left under the altar. It is said that they were once owned and worn by St Paul.

I did make a hole outside the gate, and buried them in a leather bag. To mark the place I planted a young tree. Then I escaped, and after many wanderings I came to Ireland.'

Dad put the book on the the table and smiled with pleasure at the look of astonishment on the faces of his children.

'Wow!' gasped Simon, looking at the little cross that hung from his neck. 'This was actually owned by a saint!'

'And he wore this ring,' said Sandy in a hushed voice as she slipped it on her finger. 'What a find!'

Ding said, 'I wonder what happened to the monk who hid them and wrote the book?'

'We know the answer to that as well,' replied the doctor. 'He died in Ireland soon after writing the book, but he didn't say which monastery it was, and historians have been trying to find out ever since. The monastery, we know now, was actually here where we are sitting. So, only the few of us know the secret.'

The children wanted to keep the secret to themselves. Ding said she thought their finds should be reported to the police. The doctor said that because it was gold it was probably treasure – and half should go to the Government.

The children were shocked to hear this.

'But, Dad,' said Simon, '*we* found it.'

'And in our garden,' added Sandy.

Eventually they all agreed to keep the secret to themselves, as their father put it, 'for the time being', and, as Ding cooked the supper, they began to decorate the Christmas tree. As Sandy draped the silver tinsel over the branches, she saw, floating in front of her, a picture of the opening of a cave; stretched from side to side, blocking the entrance were strings of sparkling tinsel like a beautiful spider's web. The picture disappeared as she heard her father say, 'Sandy, stop day-dreaming and please pass me the fairy to put on top.'

'Well, Dad,' she smiled at her father, 'it was a very beautiful dream.' She was to remember this much later in another land.

Before long they had finished decorating the tree and the room and it was time for bed.

The children kissed their father and Ding goodnight and were soon upstairs in their beds. They always kept the door between their rooms open so that they could talk before going to sleep.

Sandy told Simon what had happened to her on the ladder and how frightened she had been.

Simon thought for a while. 'Perhaps it's a magic ring,' he said.

'Yes, and I think it's a magic cross,' said Sandy, 'because as soon as you touched it all the frightening things stopped. Are you wearing it now, Simon?'

'Yes, I'll always wear it,' he replied sleepily.

Sandy gave a great yawn — she was very tired — snuggled down under her duvet and closed her eyes.

'I'm wearing the ring too,' she said, and just before falling asleep she eased it round and down on to her finger to make sure it wouldn't come off in the night.

She felt a soft breeze blowing her hair onto her cheeks so that it tickled. She sniffed and smelt a wood fire, and heard men talking quietly nearby. She put out a hand and felt something soft and wet. It was a little white lamb curled beside her. She was lying out in the open under the stars, covered with a rough blanket. Then quite clearly she heard one of the men say, 'I just can't understand why the Romans want to count everyone; I've never known Bethlehem so full of people!'

Chapter Three

Sandy pinched herself to make sure that she wasn't dreaming. She shut her eyes tightly, counted five, and then opened them. Everything was the same: the stars, the lamb, the people round the fire. To make quite sure she put out her hand again to the lamb, who gently pushed a wet nose into it and then tried to suck one of her fingers.

She lay back and decided to 'have a think'. Whenever she had a problem, or worry, or trouble, she would try and go to a quiet place, and just sit and 'have a think'. She would think hard about the problem and try to make a plan for solving it.

'The first thing to decide,' she thought to herself, 'is how did I get here and where am I? I remember talking to Simon. We were both in bed at home. I was feeling sleepy, and I made sure the ring was on my finger. And that's the last thing I remember.'

She touched the ring on her finger and was happy to feel it was still there. Somehow she knew that as long as she was wearing the ring she could safely get back home. She didn't know how, but she was surprised that she wasn't feeling frightened or worried at all.

'Now, the second question,' she said to herself, 'is where exactly am I? The man who spoke just now said something about the Romans and Bethlehem, and . . .'

She sat up with such a jerk that the lamb went flying off the blanket, and one of the men lying nearby turned and said to her, 'Go to sleep, girl, you've got a long walk tomorrow.'

She lay back, and the lamb staggered and wobbled onto the blanket again, and nudged into her middle where it was warm.

'Good gracious,' she whispered to herself, 'I must be outside Bethlehem with the shepherds!'

She still wasn't frightened. She felt as if she knew them and had been with them before. She could even remember some of their names, and how she had been given the lamb by the shepherds to look after. And tomorrow she was to return with it to Herod's palace in Jerusalem.

Thinking back still farther she remembered how Silas, who was Herod's chief steward, had told her that morning to go to the shepherds who were looking after the king's sheep near Bethlehem. She was to ask them for a pure white lamb for one of Herod's ceremonies in the temple. She had walked the five miles to Bethlehem, and there, under a tree, she had eaten the food the kitchen maid had given her for the journey. After asking the way, (the town was full of people who all seemed to know where the king's shepherds were), she turned east and soon found them watering the sheep in a stream near a small grassy plain.

When she had told the head shepherd that she had been sent from the palace for a lamb for sacrifice, he had taken a long time to find one that was suitable. Then after the sheep had been safely guided into the stone enclosure for the night, they had all eaten an evening meal, and after prayers had been said they lay down to sleep round the fire.

'But all this *can't* happen to me,' thought Sandy. 'This morning I was at home, and Old Dutch fell down, and we found the old cross and the ring. Then Dad told us how they had come to be under the tree. How can I be in two places at once at different times; and not only that, but also be two different people?'

Now she was feeling a little bewildered. She wished Simon was with her so that she could talk to him. He could always explain things clearly to her. She didn't want to leave the shepherds, but it *would* be a comfort to know that she *could* go back home if she wanted to. After all, she thought, they will all be wondering where I've gone to when they see my empty bed, and Simon will be worried because I've gone away without saying goodbye to him.

By now she was getting quite worked up, so she decided to 'have a think' again. I must keep calm, she thought to herself. If only I can understand how I got here, I'm sure I can get back. Then she remembered that as she was falling asleep in her bed she had twisted the ring round and round her finger. 'This *must* be the way,' she thought excitedly, 'because on the ladder I moved it only half round, and this was why everything went wrong. It has to be twisted round and round as fast as possible! Then I am moved into a different place in a different time. Simon was right. It *is* a magic ring!'

She decided to try it. She closed her eyes. With the forefinger and thumb of her right hand she turned it round and round on the finger of her left hand as fast as she could. It didn't seem to work at first, although the pillow of grass she had made for head seemed to be softer for some reason. She opened her eyes. It was very dark, and the stars had disappeared. The clouds must be coming over she thought, I hope it's not going to rain. She turned her head, and instead of looking at the dying fire she could see dimly the outline of her bedroom window. She was back in her own bed!

She gave a shriek of joy, jumped out of bed and

rushed into Simon's room. In the darkness she nearly tripped over his slippers and something else he had left lying on the floor. She gave another shriek, and reaching his bed, shook him as hard as she could. Simon was soon awake, and he wasn't at all pleased about being woken up in such a rough manner. He thought the house must be on fire, or something like that.

'What is it, Sandy?' he said, turning on his bedside light.

'I've come back!' she said, expecting to give him a big surprise.

'Where have you been?' he said, with a long sigh.

'Well,' she said, 'You won't believe it, but I've been with the shepherds outside Bethlehem!'

She was going to start at the beginning and tell him everything until she got to the end.

'Sandy, you've been dreaming. Do go back to bed and let me go to sleep.' He turned off the light and turned over.

'Simon, *please*! I promise!'

This was a word she only used to him when something was really serious. He turned the light on again and looked at her.

'All right,' he said, 'Tell.'

They both lay down under the duvet, and this time she told him everything. How she turned the ring round before falling asleep. How she had found herself with the shepherds, and how she remembered being sent to fetch the lamb by the chief steward of King Herod in the palace of Jerusalem.

Simon became more and more excited as she went on describing how beautiful Jerusalem was, and how she was a servant girl, but everyone was kind to her.

'So it *is* a magic ring,' he said.

'It must be,' replied Sandy, 'and your cross must be magic as well.'

Simon looked at his cross, still hanging from his neck.

'I can't turn it round and round,' he said, 'but it seems that just touching it guards the person who wears the ring from danger.' Then he had an idea.

'Why don't we both go back together?' he said. 'If I hold on to you while you twist the ring it might take us both back.'

Sandy had a quick think. 'That would be great!' she exclaimed. 'I've got to be back in Jerusalem tomorrow with the lamb . . .' Suddenly she stopped, aghast at what she had just realised.

'Simon,' she whispered, 'Do you remember what happened at Bethlehem years and years ago?'

Simon realised what she meant, and he too was so surprised at the thought of it that he just looked at her in astonishment.

'Jesus was born in Bethlehem,' he whispered back.

Neither said anything for a long time. Then Simon said quietly what they had both been thinking. 'We may actually see Him!'

'Of course,' said Sandy, 'and the angels told the shepherds where to find him. If we go back we could go with them!'

By now they were both so sleepy that, although they went on talking excitedly, they found it more and more difficult to think clearly.

Their father found them in the morning curled up under Simon's duvet, so fast asleep that he found it difficult to wake them. It was not often that he became angry, but now he was so annoyed with them that he gave them each a hard slap where it hurt most.

'Ding has had your breakfast ready for half an hour,' he told them, 'And why are you sleeping together? I told you before that these duvets are not big enough for two, and you'll both get colds. I'm late for surgery. I'll be back for tea so that we can finish the Christmas tree together.'

He bent over and kissed them both, and they put their arms round his neck and wouldn't let him go. He enjoyed it for a few moments, and then escaped by tickling them under their arms.

As soon as he had gone the children looked at each other. Each knew what the other was thinking. They were going to try to get back together to see the baby Jesus. Instead they had fallen asleep!

'We can't go back now,' said Simon. 'Ding will miss us and there will be an awful lot of trouble for Dad if we disappear. We'll have to wait until tonight.'

'But it's Christmas Eve today,' said Sandy, laughing as she jumped out of the bed and rushed to her room to get dressed. 'We'll be in time after all. It's *tonight* that the angels come to the shepherds.'

'You're right, *of course* it is!' shouted Simon through the door. 'We'll come up to bed early so that we are not late.' He thought this sounded so funny that he said it over and over again, until Sandy threw a pillow at him and they both ran downstairs laughing.

The morning passed slowly, as time always does when you want it to go quickly.

Outside, a heavy rain had melted all the snow, and although it was still drizzling, men had arrived in a lorry and were busy cutting up Old Dutch with power-saws. It upset the children to see the old tree being cut up and carted off. The noise was so loud that when the rain stopped after lunch they decided to walk to the town to buy last-minute Christmas presents.

All the way to the shops they chatted about the magic ring and Sandy's trip back to Bethlehem. 'We don't know for sure,' said Simon 'that it *is* the time for Jesus to be born in Bethlehem.'

'But it's Christmas Eve,' said Sandy. 'He was born tomorrow on Christmas Day.'

'I know,' replied Simon, 'I'm not stupid, you know.' (He had got into the habit of saying this far too often and his father was trying to tease him out of it.) 'But how do we know that when we go back it will be the Christmas Eve when Jesus was born? It could be any Christmas before or afterwards.'

'Well, if it was before or afterwards it wouldn't be the real Christmas when he was born, would it?' she replied. She was beginning to get muddled herself now. Suddenly she stopped, and closed her eyes.

'I *know* it's the right one, because Bethlehem was full of people and when I asked what was happening, someone told me that Quirinius had ordered that everyone must be registered in his own home town so the Romans could collect more taxes. The town was so full that people were wandering around looking for a place to stay the night.

'Who was Quirinius?' asked Simon.

'He was Governor of Syria,' said Sandy, 'And the other day he came to the palace and had a meal with King Herod. I was in the kitchen, of course, but I saw him arrive, and I saw him leave with his mounted escort. And this is what happened when Jesus was born. This is why He was born in a stable. There was no room for them in the hotel because so many had come to be counted.'

Simon looked at her in admiration.

'We shall see Him, Sandy,' he said with growing excitement. 'If you can take me back with you tonight we shall see Him!'

Chapter Four

The town was crowded with people buying their last-minute presents before the Christmas holidays. There was a traffic jam in the high street. Cars were honking their hooters. Everyone was in a rush to finish their shopping and get home.

The children turned into the big store, and after they had bought the gifts they wanted, they went up the escalator to the record bar for a drink. Sitting on the stool next to Simon was a school friend called Peter. Peter introduced a girl to him as Jo. Above the loud pop music, Jo said to Sandy what a beautiful ring she was wearing, and please could she look at it? Sandy didn't really want to take it off. She looked at Simon, imploring him with her eyes to help, but when she saw that he couldn't do anything, she took the ring off and held it up. Jo took it from her, said how pretty it was with the fish engraving, slipped it on her finger and immediately began to turn it round slowly.

Simon and Sandy looked at each other in horror, expecting to see her disappear in front of them. Then everything happened very quickly. Jo started to roll about as if she were drunk. She put her hands over her ears and started to scream. Quickly Sandy looked hard at Simon and put her hand to her neck, willing him to do the same. He read the message and touched the cross immediately. At this instant Jo returned to normal, smiled at them, apologised for 'feeling a little faint' and returned the ring to Sandy.

Simon grabbed Sandy by the arm. 'Let's get out of here!' he shouted in her ear. He edged her to the door and they waved goodbye to their friends. Soon they were out on the street and on their way home.

'Thank heavens she didn't turn the ring round any faster,' said Sandy, 'She might have disappeared right in front of us, and then we should have had some explaining to do!'

'Yes, and we now know one thing for certain,' replied Simon, 'The cross defends whoever is wearing the ring.'

'And as *that's* going to be only *me* in future,' laughed Sandy, 'I hope that you won't forget!'

When they reached home it had begun to snow again, and it was nearly dark. They were glad to get into the warm house and were soon helping Ding to finish the decorations.

They found it difficult to contain the excitement they felt about the adventure that lay before them that night. They were bursting to tell Ding and their father all about it, but they knew that they would either not be believed, or if they were believed, somehow they would be stopped from going.

'I wonder if we should leave a note in case anything goes wrong,' said Sandy, thinking aloud. She had forgotten that Ding was nearby helping with the tree.

Ding looked at them both. 'Now what exactly are you two up to?' she said. 'Pass me that star please, Simon.' She climbed on a chair and fixed the star in place, and whilst she was doing this Simon was able to whisper to Sandy, 'Don't worry, nothing can go wrong as long as I've got the cross.'

Luckily Ding appeared to have forgotten what Sandy had said, and when Dad returned, they were all so busy hanging paper chains and wrapping presents that the time seemed to fly by, and it was the children who suggested that it was time they went to bed.

'Ho! ho!' said Dad, looking at them both very carefully. 'Going to bed early on Christmas Eve? Now I wonder just what the reason for that could be. I think something must be cooking.'

The children looked at each other.

'There's nothing cooking, Dad,' said Simon, covering his mouth with his hand and pretending to yawn, 'We're just tired.'

'All right,' said Dad, 'I don't want you to be late for church tomorrow morning. We leave here at nine o'clock. Don't forget to hang up your stockings for Father Christmas.'

Ding gave them a stocking each and kissed them goodnight before they went upstairs to bed.

After they had finished their baths, their father came up and said prayers with them, kissed them goodnight and turned off the light. As soon as he had gone Simon went through to Sandy's bed.

'Right,' said Sandy, 'Off we go. I only hope it works. Hang on to my arm with both hands. Are you ready?'

Simon wasn't really ready. There was so much he wanted to ask her about what he should do when they found themselves in another place. What would happen if they couldn't speak the language? And then, he thought, we can't even be sure that we will be going to Bethlehem: we could land up in the arena in Rome being eaten by lions!

'Simon, are you ready?' repeated Sandy.

'Yes, I think so,' said Simon.

She felt Simon grip her tightly, and she shut her eyes and turned the ring round and round.

The change this time was much more gradual. They seemed to be floating on their backs on a cushion of air. It was really a lovely feeling. Simon was still holding on to Sandy, although he couldn't see her, and they were both hoping it would last a long time when suddenly the floating ceased, and the ground they were lying on felt very hard. A lamb bleated, and they felt a movement between them on top of the blanket that covered them. They opened their eyes and saw above them thousands of stars pin-pricked across the sky from one side to the other.

'We're back,' whispered Sandy. She lifted the lamb and felt the soft wool against her cheeks. Then she looked around. 'It's exactly as it was when I left,' she said.

Simon sat up and scratched his head. 'It's coming back to me now,' he said. 'I'm a servant-boy in the High Priest's house and you're a servant-girl in King Herod's palace. I was sent to find a lamb for a sacrifice in the temple and so we both came to Bethlehem together.'

He scratched his head again and tried to think back before that. 'Don't you remember, Sandy, our parents died when we were very small, so we had to find work?'

'Of course I remember,' she replied, 'but it's all so puzzling. Which is our real life, this here or the one at home with Dad and Ding?'

He thought hard for a moment. 'I think they are both real, but the life at home must be the important one because it was there we found the cross and the ring which helps us come from one to the other. You have got the ring, haven't you?' he asked anxiously.

'Of course,' she replied, holding out her hand, 'I shall never take it off.'

Suddenly she had a moment of panic. 'You have got the cross?' she asked.

He drew back the folds of the rough, (and rather dirty) tunic he was wearing, and there it was, hanging round his neck.

The lamb started to bleat again and they both sat up and looked round. The shepherds were sitting round a small fire cooking their evening meal. One of them called out, 'Come over here, Simeon, and tell your sister to bring the lamb for feeding.'

'They always call me Simeon,' he said, throwing off the blanket.

They stood up and Sandy picked up the lamb. 'They call me Sarndi,' she said. Simon put his arm round her. 'Come on,' he smiled. 'Let's go.'

When they reached the fire, the oldest of the men, (who had a very kind face), told Sandy to take the lamb to its mother and leave it there for feeding. Then he motioned Simon with his hand to sit down. He handed him a bowl of soup and some bread. When Sandy returned she was given the same. She was not expected to sit in the same circle with the men and she sat slightly behind Simon.

After they had all finished eating, a short thanksgiving prayer was said, and some other shepherds came over and sat down round the fire. One of them spoke to Simon.

'You tell the High Priest there's not a lamb to be had,' he said, 'at least not fit for sacrifice. Your sister has taken the last one for the King. There may be one at the end of the month. And be you gone back to Jerusalem tomorrow morning.'

The old man with the kind face who was King Herod's chief shepherd spoke to Sandy.

'Tell the steward he's lucky to have a lamb at this time of the year, especially a pure white one. I don't know what's going on in Jerusalem,' he went on, talking to no one in particular, 'wanting lambs at this time of the year. I do hear there's more talk of a Messiah coming very soon.'

'Aye,' said another, 'There's wild talk in Bethlehem about the coming of the Messiah. A Saviour to throw the Romans back into the sea!' He laughed. 'Can you imagine it? He would have to be stronger than Goliath, richer than King Herod and braver than King David.'

'And have more brains than all of them put together,' laughed the youngest shepherd. 'Although I don't suppose Goliath had many brains; but can you imagine such a man?'

The other shepherds joined in the laughter. The old man held up his hand. 'Don't forget,' he said quietly, 'that not only have the prophets told us that he is to be of the family of David, but also that he

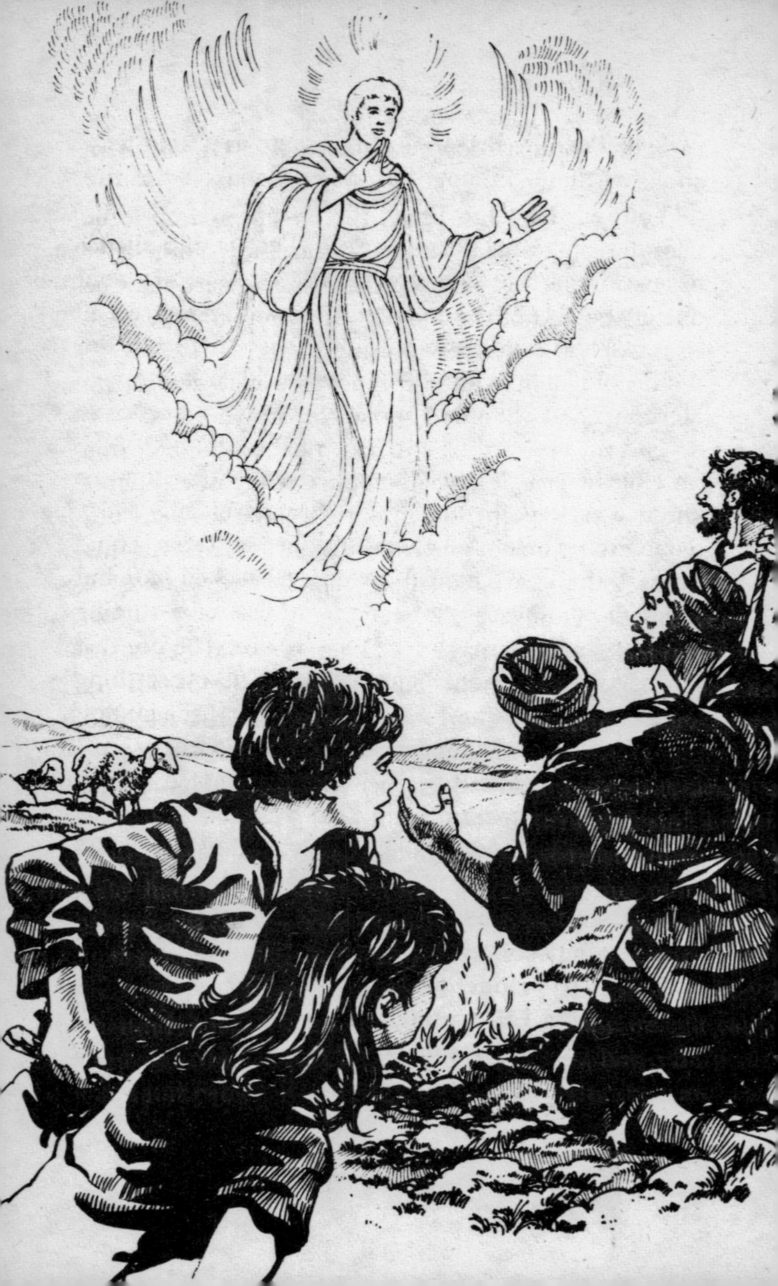

will be born in Bethlehem, the same as David was.' He turned to Simon. 'Put more wood on the fire, boy.'

It was then that they heard it. That is, if a silence *can* be heard. The cool breeze stopped. The fire went on burning but made no noise at all. The sheep all stopped bleating. It was so suddenly so silent and still that the children thought the world had stopped going round. None of them had ever felt a silence so silent.

Then he was there before them. Somehow he seemed to be both in the clouds and yet only a few feet from them. Afterwards none of them could describe exactly what the head angel looked like, but they all agreed on two things. He was of a shining brightness they had never seen anywhere before that lit up all the ground before them. The other thing they remembered was his face, which was the kindest and gentlest and most beautiful they had ever seen.

At first they were all very very frightened. Sandy moved closer to Simon and held his hand.

The head angel spoke very softly, and his voice was like music.

'Do not be afraid,' he said, 'I have good news for you; there is great joy coming to everyone. Today in David's city a Saviour has been born to you – the Messiah, the Lord. And this is your sign: you will find a baby lying wrapped in his swaddling clothes, in a manger.'

And then, wherever they looked, in the sky and round about them, they saw angels, hundreds and hundreds of them, all singing and praising God.

By now the shepherds and children had lost all their fear, and as they all stood gazing with amazement at the wonderful sight which surrounded them, the heavenly music seemed to swell louder and louder, and all together the angels sang with great joy, 'Glory to God in highest heaven, and on earth His peace, His favour towards men.'

Then, as slowly as the stars go out at dawn, they all began to disappear, and the music and singing started to fade, until once more the shepherds, the children and the sheep were left with a silent night.

Chapter Five

With their mouths wide open, and in the silence broken only by the bleating of the sheep, they went on standing and looking up at the sky for, perhaps, three minutes. Then they all looked at the old man as he stood holding on to his shepherd's staff. Tears were running down his cheeks, but his face was lit up with joy. 'He has come!' he said to them, 'He has come at last! Praise to the God of Moses, the God of David, and the God of Israel! He has come as a new-born babe!'

Simon and Sandy looked at each other. For a long time neither of them could speak. Then Simon let out a long sigh. Sandy looked up again into the sky hoping that the angel would come back, although she knew that he had finished his message.

Now all was hustle and bustle, movement and chatter, as they prepared to leave for Bethlehem to look for the new-born baby. Overnight cooking pots were removed from the fires and the fires put out. Blankets and belongings were left near the gate of the sheep enclosure. It was unthinkable that any one of them should be asked to stay behind with the sheep; they would have to leave them under God's protection.

The old man, the King's shepherd, was urging them to hurry. He told Sandy to bring her lamb with her as she could return it to Jerusalem after seeing the baby. She ran to the small enclosure where the ewes were kept, climbed over the stone wall and lifted the lamb up to Simon. Simon put it round his neck, (like putting on a warm school scarf), holding its back legs in his left hand and its front legs in his right. Quickly they followed the shepherds down the little path that led to Bethlehem below.

It was almost an hour's walk. The shepherds were so excited and in such a hurry to get there that the children found it difficult to keep up with them. They took it in turns to carry the lamb, which became heavier and heavier. Luckily it didn't wriggle or struggle to be put down, but Sandy was relieved when suddenly they all stopped and she was able to take a rest.

The shepherds had realised that they didn't know where to look for the baby in Bethlehem. Everyone would be asleep at that time of the night, and, as one of them said, it would be like looking for a needle in a haystack.

'The angel said we'd find Him in a manger,' said one of them.

'What's He doing in a manger?' said another.

'It doesn't matter,' said the old man, 'We shall soon know. We will take the path that goes past the caves that are used as stables. It is in my heart that we shall find Him somewhere there.'

They all started off again, and Simon carried the lamb. It was all downhill now, and soon they were approaching the town. A few dogs barked as they passed by some houses, and although with the full moon it was almost as light as day, they saw no one, until, so suddenly that it startled them, a man stood in the middle of the road as if waiting for them. As they drew nearer they saw a young man with a wide smile and laughing eyes who raised his arms to them as they stopped before him.

'I am Joseph, the son of Jacob,' he said. 'We have been expecting you. Please follow me and I will take you to the baby.'

In silence they followed him up a narrow lane and into a courtyard where they threaded their way between families sleeping on the ground around their dead fires. On the other side of the yard Joseph asked them to wait.

'I will not keep you long,' he said, 'I'll just

see if Mary is ready to meet you.'

He disappeared through a hole in the rock into the cave, but returned almost immediately and beckoned them inside.

Simon and Sandy followed them all in, and stood in wonder at what they saw. The cave was narrow and long – about fourteen yards by four. Near the entrance a cow was lying with her calf, and chickens scratched in the straw. On one side stood the family donkey nibbling some hay with a dog asleep nearby. At the far end the shepherds were all kneeling before a young girl who sat on some hay on the floor. But they were looking behind her where, carved out of the wall of the cave was a small trough, or manger, in which the food for the animals was placed. Lying on some clean soft hay was a new-born baby. He was tightly wrapped from head to foot in a small blanket, which was bound round with strips of a different cloth like a bandage – His swaddling clothes. He was fast asleep. Around His head shone a light of such magical softness and beauty that they had no doubt that they were looking at the Messiah.

The young woman rose, gently took the baby from the manger, and sat down with Him in her arms. Joseph stood behind her.

'I am Mary,' she said to them with a beautiful smile, 'and this is Jesus. You are welcome, sirs.'

The children had put the lamb between them and were both on their knees.

The old man slowly stood up with the help of his crook. He told Mary and Joseph all that had happened on the hillside, and then how they had been told by the angel to come to Bethlehem to find the baby. Then he looked around him.

'I don't rightly know how it be,' he said, scratching his head, 'A few of us poor shepherds who don't keep the law. A couple of children. A donkey, a cow, a dog and some hens. It don't seem right, but God does things His way and it's always better than ours.' He knelt on one knee once more in silent adoration to the babe, then he got up and said to Mary, 'Thank you Ma'am, we best get back to the sheep.'

Mary thanked them for their visit, and after Joseph had wished them a safe return to the hills they filed out past the children into the courtyard, singing the song which began, 'God be gracious to us and bless us'.

Simon and Sandy stood up.

'I wish we had a birthday present for Jesus,' said Sandy.

'That's just what I've been thinking,' replied Simon as he bent down to pick up the lamb.

They both looked at the lamb, and then at each other.

'*Of course*,' whispered Sandy, 'I can find another one to give Silas.'

They moved forward and knelt before Jesus and His mother.

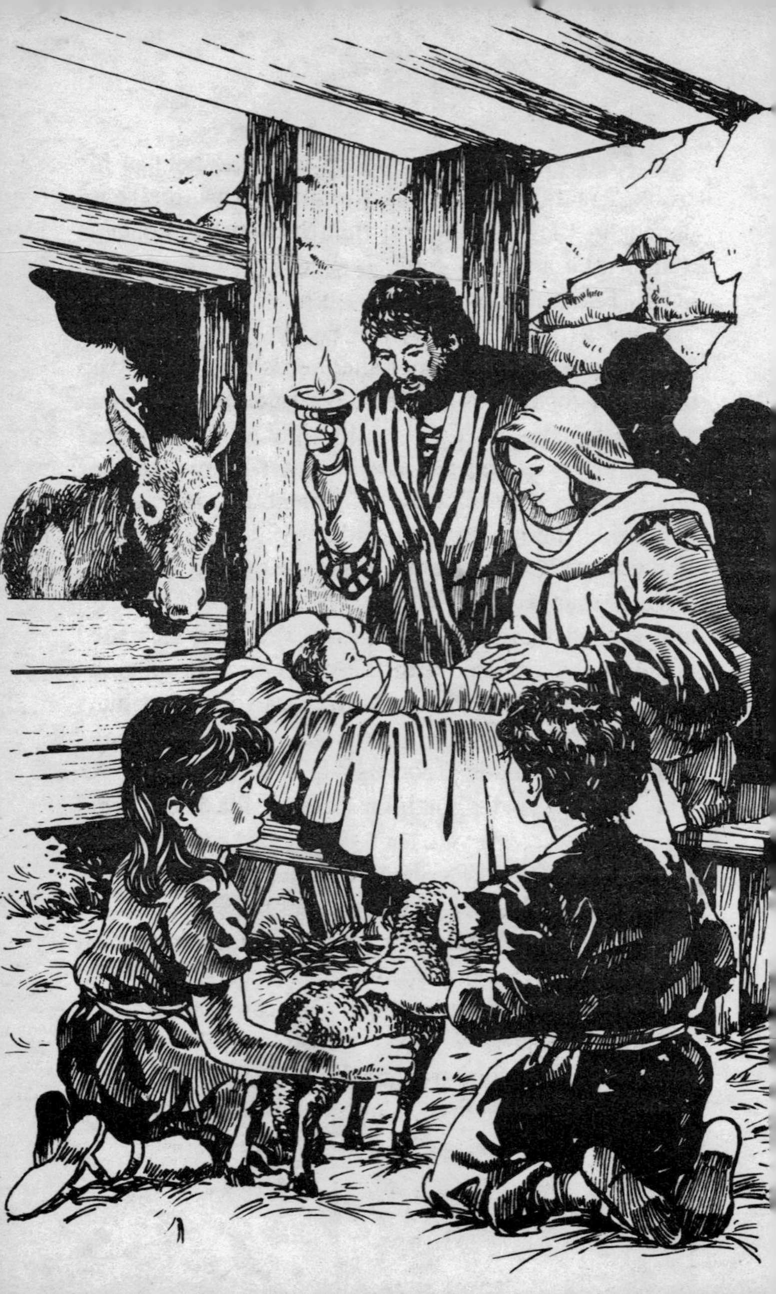

Sandy said to Mary and Joseph, 'We would like to give this lamb as a present for Jesus.' Simon laid it down gently on the hay. 'It doesn't really belong to us,' she added, 'But I am sure Silas won't mind, and we shall replace it.'

Mary put her hand on the lamb's soft coat and smiled at the children. 'Thank you,' she said, 'It shall grow up with Him, and He will remember that His first gift was from two children. And now I must feed Him, so go in peace. I have a feeling that we shall meet again.'

Joseph thanked them for their gift, led them out into the courtyard and wished them a safe journey back to Jerusalem.

It was dawn, and people were beginning to wake up and move about. The children bought a long length of sugar cane each from a stall in the town, and set off along the dusty road to Jerusalem, chewing the cane as they walked.

They reached the half-way stone as the sun began to get hot, and sat down for a rest under the shade of a fig tree. Simon had gone to get some water from a nearby spring. Sandy was wishing that she had her bicycle. She was smiling to herself at the thought of how surprised people would be to see her ride a bicycle into Jerusalem!

Suddenly a man jumped out from behind her, seized her hand and tried to pull off the ring. She screamed and struggled. Simon ran back and jumped on the man who threw him off and then started to hit Sandy to make her open her hand so he could get the ring. Simon got up, kicked the man as hard as he could, shouting 'Stop it! Leave her alone!' But the man was strong and he gave Simon a heavy blow so that he fell again. Sandy got in one or two good kicks, but she was beginning to get weaker. Suddenly the man gave a shout of terror, let go of Sandy, and ran off as hard as he could in the direction of Bethlehem. He looked behind him only once as if all the devils in hell were after him!

Simon helped Sandy to get up, and they brushed the dust off each other. Neither of them was hurt, but Sandy had been very frightened. They were panting so heavily that for some time they couldn't speak.

'Phew!' said Sandy, 'Thanks for helping. What made him run off in such a hurry?'

Simon opened the rough shirt round his neck and took the cross in his hand. 'It was the cross,' he said, 'I just touched it and the man gave a yell and ran! I saw him in the courtyard. He must have seen your ring and followed us to steal it.'

Sandy touched her ring lovingly. 'I knew when I first saw it shining that they were made to go together,' she said. 'I wish we knew the *whole* story of the cross and the ring. I expect we shall one day.'

They drank some water and walked on towards the walled city of Jerusalem, which they could see now glinting in the sunlight ahead of them. Soon they were making their way between the crowds of people, donkeys and camels, up the hill and through the gate in the wall. There was no trouble about finding their way. They were often stopped and greeted by friends of their own age whom they knew well.

When they arrived at the High Priest's house where Simon worked, they said goodbye to each other and agreed to meet at the entrance to the palace when she heard a shout, and looked round to see Simon running towards her.

'They've thrown me out!' he gasped, 'Can you believe it?' Simon was *very* cross. 'They said that I'd been too long, and when I told them there was no lamb until the end of the month they didn't believe me. Then the High Priest came into the kitchen and asked what was going on, so I told him. He was quite decent about it and told them to leave me alone. So then I told him I had seen the Messiah!' Simon paused for breath. 'And then, and then, he went purple in the face and called me a liar. He said I was mad! He said if the Messiah had come, *he* would be the first to know about it, not a kitchen boy. Then he told me to clear out and not to come back.'

Sandy had never seen Simon so angry.

'Come on,' she said, taking his hand, 'Cool down, I'm sure I can get you a job in the palace. Then we'll be together all the time.'

Simon went on muttering all the way to the palace, and when they reached the back entrance he told Sandy that the King was a cruel and horrible man, and that he didn't want to work in the palace.

'But you won't even see the King,' said Sandy, 'You will be working with me in the kitchens. He never comes near them. *Please* Simon!'

Simon thought for a minute. 'All right,' he sighed, 'It *will* be better to be together all the time.'

Sandy told him to wait whilst she went inside to find Silas who was her friend and who would fix everything.

Simon waited for a long time, and was beginning to get worried about Sandy, when two men appeared with Sandy behind them. They were beautifully dressed as senior servants of Herod's household. They stood on the steps and looked carefully at Simon for a while. Sandy, behind them, was looking very anxious and was trying to make signals to Simon which he didn't understand. Then the men whispered together, and waved Simon to come closer. Simon moved forward and stood before them.

'You are a lucky boy,' said the one who looked as if he was Herod's chief steward, 'His Majesty King Herod's personal page died yesterday. You will take his place.'

Chapter Six

For a few seconds Simon stood frozen with fear. *Everyone* knew what a wicked man King Herod was. They said that he didn't trust anyone. They said that he had murdered hundreds of people, including his wife and some of his sons.

'Crumbs,' thought Simon. 'He probably murdered his page – and I'll be the next on the list!' He thought of making a run for it, but they would be sure to catch him, and then Sandy would get into trouble.

The chief steward put his hand on his shoulder and looked at him kindly. 'Don't worry, boy. I'll keep an eye on you. It's a good job and well paid. Your sister can share your room so that you won't be lonely. The King returns from Tiberius tomorrow. Report to me early in the morning and I'll teach you your duties.'

He went inside with the other man and the children were left on their own.

'I'm sorry,' whispered Sandy, 'I just couldn't help it. They came in when I was telling Silas about you. Then they asked lots of questions and that was that. I was trying to warn you not to refuse the job or they would have forced you and treated you like a slave.'

'Don't worry,' said Simon as they went into the back entrance of the palace. 'It will be super to be together, and now that we have the cross and the ring I'm sure nothing can harm us.'

They were given a good meal in the kitchen, and were then shown their new rooms which they were to share and which were quite close to Herod's own apartments. While they washed and put on their new clothes and sandals they chatted to each other about the day's events.

Sandy was relieved that Silas had not been angry when she had returned without a lamb. He had said that it didn't matter as the King was away. Then, as there was not much to do in the kitchens, he had given her a day's holiday.

Simon remembered that they had forgotten to register their names in the counting of people in Bethlehem, but no one seemed to worry about it. He thought how funny it would be to give their real names and addresses; they would certainly be thought quite mad.

They were still very excited about the vision of the

angels, and their visit to the stable, and could think of little else.

'I know,' said Sandy, 'Let's go and tell Simeon all about it.'

Simeon was a great friend of the children. He was very old, (Simon thought he must be nearly a hundred), and he lived by himself not far from the temple. He often told them stories from the Torah. Always he would weave into the story the certainty of the coming of the Messiah; the One whom the prophets had declared would one day come to save Israel.

Simon was bursting to tell someone about it all. No one in Jerusalem could possibly know anything about it yet, so they would be first with the wonderful news.

'Sandy, you *do* have a good idea sometimes. Shall we walk or shall we go by bus?'

They ran out of the palace laughing so much that, not looking where they were going, they ran into a squad of Roman soldiers marching up the street. The sergeant in charge halted his men, one of whom had tripped over Simon and fallen down. They were all very angry, and one of them grabbed Simon and hit him hard on the head. The sergeant only let the children go after Simon had said he was *very* sorry several times.

'Blasted Romans!' he muttered, as they stood watching the soldiers march on. 'They shouldn't be here. This isn't their country!'

'Hush, Simon,' whispered Sandy, wishing the soldiers would move off a little faster before Simon really got them into trouble. 'After all, they *have* conquered it, and *they* put troops in the castle for six months. I heard that it was with Herod's agreement because he is expecting trouble.'

But soon they had recovered, and were hurrying along the narrow streets to Simeon's house.

They climbed some rough stone steps and found him sitting on the flat roof of his house reading Isaiah. He was delighted to see them again and called his servant for lemonade and cakes. After hearing the news about Simon's new job at the palace, Simeon looked grave.

'Look after yourselves, my children,' he said. 'Be *very* careful. They say that King Herod is mad, and one never knows what a mad person is going to do next.

It was then they told him that they had a wonderful surprise for him. For a little while they teased him. They asked him who he was expecting to come, and when he replied that he had few visitors they said the name began with M or J. Only when they saw that he was getting tired did they tell him simply that they had seen the Messiah, and that His mother had called Him Jesus.

The effect on him was astonishing. Slowly he stood up and closed his eyes; then he asked them to tell him the whole story from the beginning to the end. While he stood they told him everything, and when they had finished, he opened his eyes and looked up at the sky.

'Praise be to God!' he said, 'Yes, it must be Him. Jesus the Saviour! Soon they will bring Him to the temple and I shall see Him before I die.'

He sat down, and as he seemed quite lost in his thoughts, or perhaps his prayers, the children left him and crept quietly into the street.

Now, if at this point they had returned to the palace, they would not have soon found themselves prisoners in the dungeon of the Castle Antonia, the castle which stood behind the temple and which towered over the whole area as a grim reminder that Israel was ruled by the Romans, and not by the Israelites. But the market near the outer court of the temple was always an exciting place to visit and they knew many of the stall holders who sold animals and birds for sacrifice. They liked to watch the strange foreign pilgrims from far-away countries, who had to change their money with the money-changers before they could buy things. Usually they met friends of their own age there because it was a good place to buy sweetmeats.

As the sun was rapidly sinking below the wall of the city, they hurried, and began to run. They knew the shops and stalls would close the second the sun disappeared finally over the hills to the west. Round the corner they ran into some friends from the High Priest's household who wanted to know why Simon had left. The children told them, and then enjoyed their amazement as they told them all that had happened with the shepherds at Bethlehem. Simon, who was still smarting from the blow the Roman soldiers had given him, was just telling them with great glee how the Romans would be swept into the sea, when suddenly two men sprang from behind the cart and grabbed both the children.

'So,' said the one who held Simon, twisting his arm behind his back, 'so we are to be driven into the sea, are we? And by a Messiah who is, no doubt, another rebel leader!'

'The sergeant will be interested to hear this,' said the man holding Sandy. 'You will both come with us to the castle.' He looked at his companion. 'Don't let go of him, Julius. We mustn't lose them.'

By now the other children had melted away, and with their arms gripped firmly by the two men, (they were Roman soldiers in plain dress) the children were taken up the hill and into the castle.

Simon had been too surprised to do anything, and Sandy was feeling very frightened. As they entered the gateway of the castle their fears increased. It was dark, and as they were pushed into the guard room she thought she heard a scream from somewhere below them.

Soldiers were lying about all over the floor, some

polishing their equipment, some playing dice or cards. They took no notice of the children. A soldier entered and whispered to the men holding them. They were taken out, along a passage to a small room on the right and pushed through the entrance. Behind the table facing them sat a centurion, in full uniform, except for the helmet which was on the table. He looked very surprised to see the children standing before him, and was about to ask his secret policemen if they hadn't anything better to do than arrest children, when the one holding Simon spoke.

'Excuse me sir, I know what you're thinking, but you know the old man Simeon we've been keeping a check on for some time?' The centurion nodded. 'Well, shortly after one of the zealots from Galilee slipped out of his house we saw these children go in, so we followed them. They talked with the old man on the roof. We couldn't hear everything, but they passed a message to him that the Saviour of the Jews that they had been waiting for had arrived in Bethlehem.

The centurion, who up to now had been reading a scroll and showing no interest, jumped up in great excitement.

'Go on, you idiot! Don't stop. What happened next?'

'We followed them outside, and along the street we found them telling a bunch of kids how the Saviour would throw us Romans out of Israel and into the sea!'

The centurion gloated at the children as if he had

caught a big fish. 'By all the gods, Julius, you've done well. This is what I've been waiting for!' he shouted. 'We find this man, this Saviour, and the whole movement against us will collapse like a pack of cards. He's *sure* to come to Jerusalem some time, and we've got Him! Watch Simeon's house day and night till further orders.' He came round the table and stood over the children.

'Right. Where did you see Him? How tall is He? How old! What was He wearing? Where's He from?'

Simon edged over and put his hand in Sandy's. 'Don't say a thing,' he whispered. A blow on the side of the head sent him rolling across the floor. He saw stars all round him. He managed to stagger to his feet and return to Sandy's side.

The centurion was now pulling Sandy's hair savagely. She screamed. 'Speak child!' he shouted angrily. 'Answer my questions!'

Simon was now being held tightly by Julius and the other man. Desperately he reached for the cross, tearing open his shirt at the neck to reach it with his free hand. This was the only way he could save Sandy. He felt round his neck frantically. He couldn't believe it. It wasn't there!

Sandy was determined not to say anything, in spite of the pain. Simon kicked out at the centurion who was still pulling her hair to make her talk. He turned and gave Simon another blow in the face. Sandy picked up the heavy helmet with both hands and threw it at the centurion's head. It missed him and crashed against the wall. By now he had had enough.

'Take them down and lock them in the dungeon for the night to cool,' he gasped. 'We'll *make* them talk tomorrow.' He picked up his helmet and looked at the broken plume. Then for a good half-minute he looked at the children. 'And show them my special room on the way. That will make them think!'

The children were dragged down the long passage to some stone steps, where the men took lighted torches from brackets on the wall. Down the steps, (Simon counted twenty-eight), and along another narrow passage they halted. Except for the light from the oil torches it was quite dark. The men lifted their torches high.

'Take a good look at the special room,' chuckled Julius.

The children gasped with horror as they looked through a narrow split in the stone wall into the room. Tied to a high beam by their wrists three men were hanging in a row, just dangling like carcasses of meat from a meat hook. One of the men was moaning, and one looked as if he were dead. Round the walls were horrible instruments of torture.

Simon quickly put his hand over Sandy's eyes so that she wouldn't see, but it was too late, she had seen everything.

'Move on,' said Julius, giving them a push. 'Your cell is next door.'

A little further on at the end of the passage he opened a heavy wooden door with a large key.

'Get in,' he said gruffly.

They were both flung forward into the darkness. Behind them the door creaked once and then slammed shut. They heard the key turn in the lock, and the footsteps die away along the passage and up the steps. Then all was quiet in the cell except for the moaning of the men hanging next door, and the scurrying of rats over the floor.

Chapter Seven

They stood for a while, holding hands in the darkness without saying anything. The moaning died away. A rat climbed on to Sandy's foot. She gave a shudder and kicked it off. It scurried away making angry little screeching noises.

'The cross,' said Sandy, still holding Simon's hand. '*Why* didn't you use the cross?'

'I've lost it,' replied Simon miserably. 'I'm sorry Sandy. It must have dropped off when the sergeant knocked me down.' He sounded so upset that Sandy put her arms round him and gave him a hug.

'Don't worry,' she said, 'I'm sure we shall get it back. But first we *must* get out of here. Don't say anything. I'm going to have a think.'

Simon waited for a long time. Nothing happened.

He was just about to suggest that they hid behind the door and hit the guard over the head when he came back, when Sandy said she had got the only answer. 'There's only one way to get out of here, and that's to use the ring to get home.'

'That's what I've been thinking,' replied Simon, 'but we must warn Simeon that he is being watched. Another thing,' he went on, 'they don't know that Jesus is a baby. They think He is a man. So if Mary and Joseph bring Jesus to Jerusalem, He should be safe; but we must warn Simeon not to tell anyone.'

'How do we do that when we're back home?' said Sandy, who was beginning to get cold and cross, 'Ring him up on the telephone, or send him an air mail letter?'

As if Simon had not heard what Sandy said, he gripped her arm firmly. 'There's only one way. We've got to come back!'

'No way,' replied Sandy. 'We always arrive back from the place we left, don't we? I'm not coming back to this dungeon, that's for sure!'

'I've got an idea!' said Simon with excitement. 'If we return with some gas or something to fix the guard when he comes to get us, we could slip out and escape.'

Sandy thought for a moment. 'It might just work,' she said. 'Gas or chloroform. We could ask Dad to give us something to knock him out, and then all we've got to do is get past the guardroom without being seen.'

The children were pleased with their plan, and

decided to return home at once. They knew that no matter how long they had been away, they would somehow always return home on the same night as they left. This meant that their absence was never noticed, so they could keep the secret of where they had been.

'Hold me tight like you did before,' said Sandy, 'and let's get out of here!'

She twisted the ring round as fast as she could.

This time they arrived back, standing together in the middle of Simon's room in the dark. Although they were only wearing pyjamas it was beautifully warm. The carpet felt soft under their bare feet and, of course there were no rats. They shouted with joy to be safely home again, and after putting all the lights on, they were soon able to forget the horror of the dungeon in the joy of Christmas Morning.

Their father came in with presents while they were unpacking their stockings.

Simon undid his parcel which was quite small, hoping that it was what he wanted so badly. It was. A miniature tape recorder, a little bigger than his hand. It was really one which was used by businessmen for dictating letters, and could be carried in a pocket. He had seen it in a shop window, and after they had allowed him to try it out by talking into it and playing it back, he knew that this was what he wanted. Sandy teased him by saying that he only wanted to hear his own voice, but he showed her that by holding it close to a radio you could record music as well.

They all sat on Sandy's bed whilst she opened her parcel. She gave her usual squeal of delight when she saw that she had been given a pencil torch and a large encyclopaedia. She had seen both in a shop window, and one morning at breakfast, hinted strongly to her father that she thought they would be very useful.

After breakfast they gave their father and Ding their presents, and they all enjoyed a happy time giving, and receiving, and opening parcels until it was time to go to church.

The children sat on either side of their father, and Ding sat at the end next to Sandy. The opening hymn was 'Come All Ye Faithful'. The organ filled the church, and made it tremble with the opening bars. Then everyone burst into song. When they came to the bit about 'Come Ye to Bethlehem', Simon leaned forward and grinned at Sandy. Sandy smiled and winked back at him.

Soon they were all sitting for the sermon. Simon was wondering if the lamb they had given Jesus was all right. They had forgotten that it would need feeding. He couldn't remember if there were any ewes near the stable to provide milk.

Sandy was worrying about how they were going to escape from the dungeon when they went back that evening to warn Simeon. She came out of her

daydream to hear the vicar say from his pulpit . . .
'And so, there were the shepherds on that cold
winter's night in the snow . . .' Before she knew
what she was doing she found that she had stood up,
and everyone was looking at her. The vicar paused in
surprise and stared at her. She felt very confused,
but she knew quite clearly that he was quite wrong.
Now everyone held their breath in astonishment at
what happened next, the vicar more than anyone. He
couldn't remember when someone had last
interrupted his sermon.

'Did you, er,' he paused, 'Did you want to say
something, Sandy?' he asked.

Sandy looked at her father, (who was too surprised
to make her sit down again), and then at all the
people. Then she turned to the vicar in the pulpit.

'Well, you see, Mr Dorman,' she said rather
meekly, 'It wasn't *very* cold and there wasn't any
snow at all!' She was going on to tell him that they
only had a fire to cook their evening meal and to
keep the wolves away, but she saw Simon making
frantic signs for her to sit down.

The vicar took out his handkerchief and blew his
nose. He couldn't think of anything else to do. He
was a kindly man and had known Sandy for years.

'Yes, well, er, thank you, my dear, thank you.'

She sat down and looked at her father, expecting
him to be looking very cross. Instead he smiled at
her in a puzzled sort of way.

The vicar went on with his sermon.

The children were very moved by the rest of the service. They both longed to tell everyone that they had seen it all, how beautiful and joyful it really was in the stable and on the hills near Bethlehem. But they somehow knew that if they did disclose their secret, the magic of the cross and the ring would vanish away.

When they arrived home Ding asked them to help her lay the table and prepare for the friends who were coming to share their lunch. They had hoped to get together to plan what they were going to take with them to help them escape from the castle. So it was after the guests had left, and the washing up was all finished, they were able to go up to their rooms and discuss the trip back.

They lay on the floor. Simon was talking into his tape recorder and then playing it back to listen to his own voice. Sandy was turning the pages of her new encyclopaedia, looking up chloroform.

'That's no good,' she said to Simon, 'It's a liquid that has to be sniffed. It takes too long. I'll try the poisons, but we mustn't hurt him too much. I was thinking of a spray of some kind to puff in his face while we run away.'

She turned the leaves of the book over. 'Pawn, peaches, penny, pepper . . .'

Simon broke in, 'Sandy, poison is spelt P-O-I-S-O-N, not P-E. Wait!' he exclaimed. 'What was the last one you said?'

Sandy said she was working her way through the P's, and it was pepper.

'That's it!' said Simon. 'Dad said the other day that one could separate the biggest and fiercest dogs in the world from fighting together by throwing pepper over them. If we throw a handful of pepper at his face when he opens the door we could grab his keys, lock him in, and run!'

Sandy looked at her brother in admiration. 'It's *got* to work,' she said. 'I don't know where you get the brains from!'

Downstairs in the kitchen they found a large glass jar labelled, 'PURE WHITE PEPPER'. They put it all into a brown paper bag and replaced the jar on the shelf.

Back in their room they discussed what else they should take with them.

'I'm sure we can only take with us what we can actually hold in our hands,' said Sandy. 'It's no use filling our pockets with things, because we're in different clothes when we arrive back.'

Simon was disappointed. In addition to his tape recorder, he wanted to take one of his father's cigars for old Simeon; also his bicycle which he thought would give him great fun, showing it off all round Jerusalem.

Sandy told him not to be stupid. She said that he had to hold on to her with one hand, so he could only take his recorder in the other, and nothing else.

In the end, because Sandy had two hands free, they agreed that she should take her pencil torch and the pepper in one hand, and a long length of nylon cord (which Ding had bought for a clothes line), in the other. This was in case they wanted to escape from anywhere else, or in case the 'pepper plan' failed.

After tea in the sitting room, the doctor sat back in his armchair and lit his pipe. When he had finished puffing out the smoke, he looked at Simon.

'I see Sandy is still wearing her ring, but I can't see your cross, Simon,' he said.

Simon blushed, and tried to think quickly what he was going to say to his father. 'Well, actually – I've lost it.' Then he added quickly, 'But I think I know where it is.'

'Where?' said Dad.

Simon looked at Sandy for help. He longed to tell his father everything, especially as they were going back into danger, but Sandy was moving her hand from side to side.

'Well, I'm not *absolutely* sure,' he replied, trying to get out of telling a lie.

The children's father decided not to ask any more about the cross. He turned to Sandy. 'How can *you* be so,' he paused to find the words he wanted, 'so absolutely sure that there was no snow near Bethlehem nineteen hundred odd years ago, Sandy?' he asked her.

Sandy looked at Simon, hoping that he would have an answer. He looked at her helplessly. She went over to her father, put her arms round his neck and kissed him. 'It's a special secret, Dad,' she said, 'and if we tell the secret we lose the magic.'

Her father thought for a moment. 'You're quite right,' he said to them both. 'Your mother always said that secrets should be kept locked up until it was time to let them out.' He got up and put his arms around them. 'Secrets can also be dangerous,' he added, 'so be careful.'

The evening passed quickly, although the children found it difficult to concentrate on the television, or the games they played after supper. They were both worried about going back without the protection of the cross. They had been warned twice now to be careful. Had it not been that Simeon was in danger, and also that Simon wanted to find his cross, they would probably not have gone back.

When at last they went up to bed, they once again felt the tingle of excitement as they stood together ready to go back into a different time and place.

With some difficulty, (because of the rope and the torch), Sandy twisted the ring round and round. This time, perhaps because she hadn't been able to turn it fast enough, the trip back was quite rough. Simon thought it was because he wasn't wearing the cross. A high wind seemed to batter them and they were engulfed by a loud noise as if they were in the middle of a storm. Then suddenly all was quiet.

They knew they were back again because of the darkness, and the rats which were climbing on to their bare feet.

Chapter Eight

Sandy dropped the rope on the floor, and as she switched on her torch the rats hurried away and disappeared into the cracks between the huge stone blocks of the walls. At the far end of the little cell they saw a narrow slit, through which a gentle breeze was blowing in the cool night air. This was the outer wall of the castle, which was also the huge defence wall that surrounded Jerusalem. There was no escape through such a narrow opening. They would have to use the pepper.

Simon picked up the rope, and after making sure the coil would not come undone, put it round his neck so that his arms were free. He put his tape recorder into the only pocket inside the loose folds of his shirt, and took the bag of pepper from Sandy.

'Turn the torch off a minute,' he whispered, 'I thought I heard something.' They stood again in the darkness and waited. Nothing happened. Not a sound. Then they heard a moan which came from the cell next to them.

'We must try and help those poor men to escape, if we can,' whispered Sandy. Simon nodded his head. He was already planning what he would do. He noticed the pale first light of dawn through the slit window. Somewhere a cock crowed. 'They could be here any time now,' he said, 'I hope only one of them comes to fetch us and not two. Quick! Give me the pepper.'

Sandy switched the torch on again and handed Simon the brown paper bag of pepper. Gently he poured as much into his right hand as he could hold. Then he gave the bag back to Sandy, and she did the same. In spite of being very careful, they both sneezed several times before they had finished. There was still some left in the bag and Sandy put this in a fold of her dress.

'You stand behind the door,' said Simon, 'when he comes in he'll be surprised to see only me. Then I shall throw the pepper in his face; then you give him your lot as well to make sure. Quickly!' he added. 'Torch off! I think he's coming.'

Again they waited, their hearts thumping like drums.

Footsteps outside. The rattle of keys. The door

creaked open and Julius came in. He stood before Simon, holding a lighted oil lamp in his left hand, the keys dangling from an iron ring on his right hand. As Simon had expected, he was astonished to see only Simon. He stood for a few seconds with his mouth open in surprise. Simon threw the pepper. A lot of it went straight into his mouth, and the rest into his face and eyes. He doubled up, dropped his lamp, and screamed.

As Sandy came from behind the door, Simon snatched the keys, and they rushed together to get out. But they only got as far as the door. Here they collided with the second gaoler who had stopped to throw some chunks of bread to the prisoners in the next cell. On hearing the scream, he rushed in to see what was happening. He knocked Simon over backwards into the cell, and then stopped in surprise when he saw Julius kneeling on the floor, his hands to his eyes, making queer animal noises.

Sandy threw her handful of pepper into his face. She grabbed Simon, and pulled him up. They dashed through the door and slammed it shut. Simon had to choose between four keys. He selected the smallest, praying that it was the right one. It was. As the key turned they heard an angry shout, and a banging on the door. They ran.

They stopped at the next cell. Sandy switched on her torch while Simon chose a key. Again it was the right one. The banging next door had stopped, but they knew they must hurry.

The men had been let down from the beam, and were lying or sitting on the floor against the wall. They had been starved and tortured, and were in poor shape. They got up slowly, frightened by the magic of Sandy's torch. The tallest of them took Simon's hand and looked into his eyes. 'My name is Dismas and these are my friends. Thank you, boy,' he said warmly. 'One day, if we get out of here, we shall repay you.'

'You must hurry!' urged Simon, 'You haven't much time.'

'Go,' replied Dismas. 'We shall manage.'

The children ran out and up the long flight of steps. As they reached the top they heard people running along the passage towards them from the direction of the guard room. They must have heard the banging, thought Simon. Quickly he undid the rope and laid it on the ground across the top step. There were two huge stone pillars on either side which supported the roof.

'Hold the other end! Hide behind the pillar!' gasped Simon. 'When I give a tug, lift it up a foot and hold it taut.'

They were only just in time. Three soldiers arrived together, running as hard as they could. Simon gave a tug and felt the rope tighten as he lifted it up. All three men tripped over it and went flying down the steps, most of the way on their heads. The children dropped the rope and ran

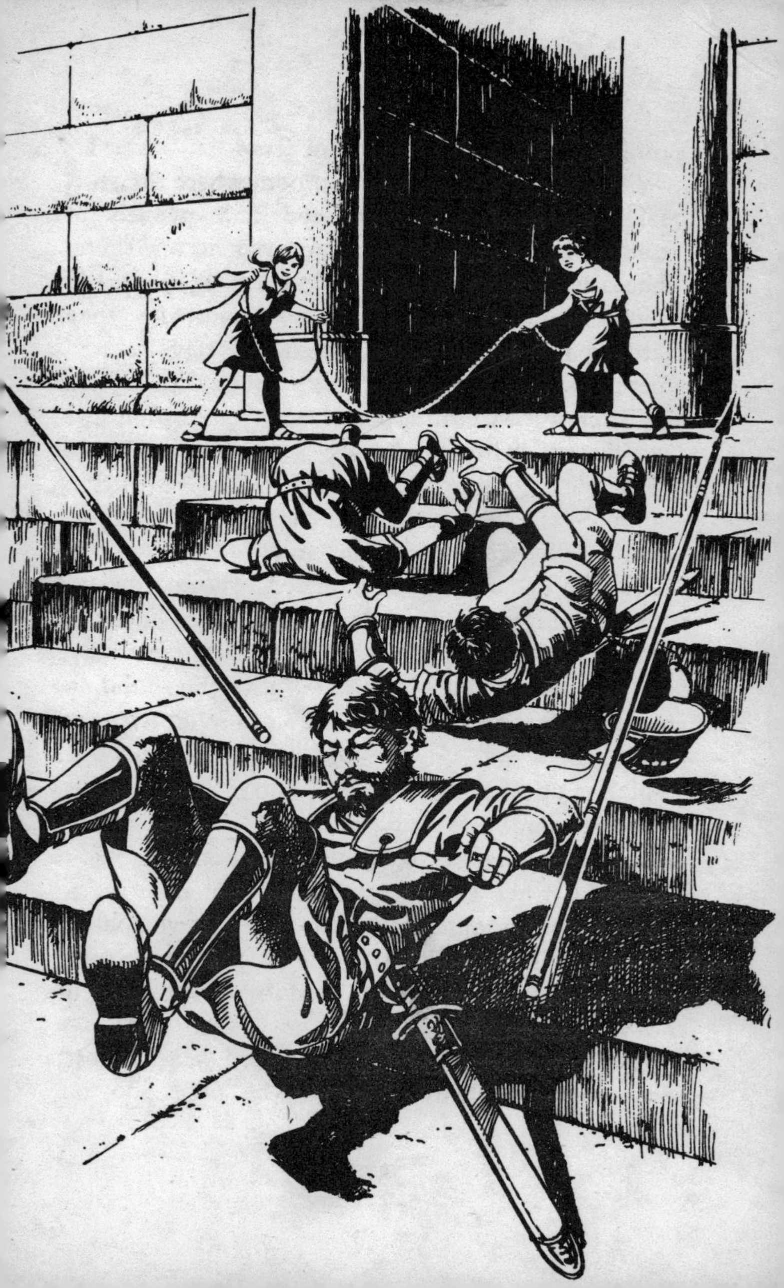

along the passage as fast as they could.

When they reached the small room where they had been questioned, they stopped and peeped in through the heavy curtain. There was no one there. The early morning sun was flooding in through a window on the outside wall. Frantically they searched for the cross. On the floor, table, everywhere. It was nowhere to be found. Simon was almost crying with disappointment. 'I *must* find it, I *must* find it!' he cried.

Sandy eventually persuaded him to give up the search. She was very frightened at the thought of being caught again inside the castle.

They walked slowly out, along past the guardroom into the courtyard. No one took any notice of them.

'Just act naturally, as if we had been visiting,' whispered Simon, 'and pass me the pepper.' Sandy gave him the bag which had about another handful left in it.

As they approached the huge gate in the wall that led to freedom, they saw two guards dressed in full uniform standing one on each side. Simon gave them a cheerful wave of his hand and, (remembering a television programme he had once seen), whispered to Sandy to keep walking on. As he drew level with them he stopped suddenly as if he had forgotten something.

'Excuse me, Sir,' he said politely to the one nearest him, 'would you like one of these?'

Romans found out that old Simeon knew who the Messiah was, they would certainly torture him to make him speak. He *must* somehow be warned not to say anything about Jesus.

Back in their rooms they talked it over. As it was not safe to go themselves, they decided to ask a kitchen lad they knew to take a message. He was to pretend to be taking a gift of fruit, and was to say to Simeon, 'Do not speak to anyone of the new baby. There is great danger.' They sent the boy off the next morning, giving him a few coins to buy fruit in the market on the way. They were never to see him again.

The King arrived in the late afternoon. He was short, fat and ugly. He swept into his apartments followed by his bodyguard, the Chief Steward (whose name was Joran), and his scribe. He stopped when he saw Simon.

'Who is this boy?' he squealed in a high-pitched voice. 'What's he doing here? Get him out!'

Simon knelt on one knee and bowed his head as he had been taught.

Joran came forward. 'He's your new page, Your Majesty,' he said with a slight bow from the waist. 'If you remember . . .' he hesitated in confusion, 'if you remember, your page died, Sire.'

Herod said nothing. He looked again at Simon, and walked on. Everyone, including Simon, followed. They passed through the huge audience chamber and many vast rooms. Everything was marble: the floors, the walls, the fountains, the statues. It was all very beautiful.

As they approached the private audience room a servant hurried up and whispered something to the steward, who in turn moved up to Herod's side and said something to him. Herod nodded his head and the steward hurried away, to return leading a man whom everyone knew as the Roman Governor who had his apartments in the castle. It was obvious that he had little respect for the puppet King, although he gave him the courtesy of a slight bow before speaking.

'As you have probably heard,' he said, looking directly into Herod's beady eyes 'Jerusalem is full of talk about the arrival of a Messiah, a new King who is going to throw us into the sea. Can you imagine what the Emperor will say when he hears this? What have you done about it?'

Herod stood up. Simon saw his eyes dart from side to side. He was frightened. Everyone knew that he was King only because it was convenient for Rome.

'I am aware of this,' he replied, as he started to pace up and down, 'and it greatly troubles me. But may I remind you, Quintus, that you are the occupying power? What have *you* done about it?' He stopped and smiled, pleased at having put the ball in the other court.

'I'll tell you what I've done about it!' replied

Quintus angrily, 'For some time we've been watching a house owned by an old man who has been waiting openly for the coming of this Messiah. Yesterday, my men arrested a young boy who was pretending to deliver fruit there. They brought him to the castle for questioning.'

Simon suddenly felt quite sick. He wanted to run, anywhere. Anywhere where he wouldn't have to hear what he feared would come next.

'Before the boy died,' went on Quintus, his voice rising louder and louder with his anger, 'he told us the message he had been given to deliver. It was about this Messiah. We couldn't get out of him who had given him the message, in spite of torturing him . . .' here he paused and waited for Herod to stop his pacing, 'but he confessed he was employed by *your* staff in the kitchen of *your* palace!'

Chapter Nine

Herod was now very frightened; he had never seen Quintus so angry. He sat down heavily, took out a large silk square and wiped the perspiration from his face. Quintus gave him a look of contempt and stalked out.

Simon was not prepared for what followed next. The King stood up and began screaming at his steward about being surrounded by traitors. Then he began to shake, and to foam at the mouth. The steward beckoned Simon over and told him to run and fetch the King's doctor. Simon ran out and found him in his room. When they returned, Herod was lying on the floor, his eyes closed, his face twitching. They carried him to his private apartments and laid him on his bed. After being given something to drink by the doctor, the King fell into what looked like a deep sleep. The doctor told Simon to call him when the King woke up. Then they all left.

Simon sat on a couch nearby and gazed at the King who was now snoring loudly. He wondered what it was that made him so evil; perhaps it was the pain of his sickness. Yet they all said he had good qualities. He had kept the peace. He had let the people off their taxes after a bad year. He had built many fine buildings. Yet he had killed so many people. Simon wondered how anyone could be so good and so bad at the same time.

'Come here, boy!'

Simon nearly jumped out of his skin. The King was awake and was looking at him. He went over and knelt on one knee.

'Can I trust you, boy?'

'Yes, Your Majesty,' replied Simon.

Herod took off his huge gold signet ring and handed it to him.

'This is your authority. You have only to show it and my orders will be carried out. Go to the High Priest and tell him to be here tomorrow at sunrise, with the priests and the scribes. Tell no one of this matter.'

Simon bowed and walked out backwards as he had been taught. Before he went through the door he saw that the King had fallen asleep again. In the long corridor he saw Sandy come out of the Queen's apartments. She had been given the rest of the day off. They agreed to go together.

The High Priest was not in his house, so they walked up the hill to the temple. In the outer court, the first person they saw was Simeon. He was sitting against the wall in the sun arguing with two men who clearly wanted him to go with them. The children looked on helplessly as they dragged him to his feet. Then Sandy had an idea.

'Use the King's ring, Simon,' she said urgently.

For a second Simon didn't know what she was talking about. Then he smiled.

'Right. Watch this,' he said. He walked over and held up his hand. 'In the name of the King you are to leave this man alone,' he said to the two men. Then because he was enjoying being so powerful, he added, 'He is now under the King's protection!'

The two men let go of Simeon and gawped at Simon. The children were both wearing the uniform of palace servants, but what made them stop instantly was the sight of the huge gold ring lying in the palm of Simon's outstretched hand. They looked at him with new respect and hurried away.

Simeon thanked them both and chuckled when they showed him the King's ring, but he was shocked to hear of the death of the young messenger they had sent him.

'Thank you,' he said. 'I received your message.

The poor lad must have been caught on his way back to you.' He sat silently for a while and then gave a sad sigh and asked them what they were doing in the temple.

When they told him all the news he made them sit down and he told them his own wonderful news.

'I have seen Jesus!' he said. His face creased in smiles as he went on, 'Yesterday they brought Him here to the temple for the ceremonies. I took Him in my arms and thanked God.' The children had never seen him look so happy. 'Now I can die in peace!'

'Where is He now?' asked Sandy.

'They returned to Bethlehem yesterday,' he replied. 'Joseph has work there and they have a house outside the town.' He placed his hands on their heads and gave them a blessing. 'Go in peace, my children, and thank you again for your help. I don't think I shall be troubled again, thanks to you.'

The children crossed the huge courtyard and Sandy had to wait in the Court of Women, as she was allowed no further. Simon went through into the Court of Men, and at the entrance to the Court of Priests showed the ring to a servant and asked for an audience with the High Priest. He had to wait some time before he appeared. He recognised Simon, and when he had heard the message he smiled. 'So now you serve the King, young man. I hope you haven't told *him* you have seen the Messiah!' He laughed. 'Go. Tell His Majesty we shall be there.'

Simon returned through the Courts and found Sandy deep in thought. She had, she said, been talking to a wonderful old woman whose name was Anna. 'She knew all about Jesus, and she saw Him here yesterday,' explained Sandy. 'But I'm frightened. So many people know about Him now. The Romans want to find Him. The King is worried about Him.' She was now on the verge of tears, 'Why are they all so frightened? He's only a baby!'

'I know,' replied Simon, as he gently led her out of the temple. 'But don't worry. They won't harm Him.'

Sandy was finding it difficult not to worry, and she suddenly wished, right there outside the temple, that her father was with them. She wanted to tell him everything, and feel his arms round her again.

'Let's go back!' she cried. 'We came to warn Simeon, and now that he's safe we can return home.'

Simon thought for a little while as they walked up the hill. He, too, was feeling a little homesick. He would have agreed there and then, but as each day went by, he was determined to find his cross. Without it, he felt that some harm would come to Sandy, and if they returned home without it, he would never see it again.

'Let's wait another day or two,' he said. '*Please*, Sandy, I do want to find my cross before we go home.'

Sandy agreed. 'All right,' she said, 'I don't know

how you're going to find it, but we'll wait another two days.'

They walked on, hand in hand, into the palace.

The next morning the King appeared to be completely recovered. He received the priests and scribes in the huge throne room, and put them at ease, laughing and joking, before coming to the reason for sending for them. He told them that he had heard of the arrival in Jerusalem of three wise men from Arabia, (which they knew already), who were looking for the newly born King of the Jews.

'Where,' he asked them, 'was this Messiah, or King, to be born?'

'In Bethlehem,' they told him, 'for so it is written in the Book of the Prophet Micah.'

Herod seemed pleased with this answer. He changed the subject, and talked about the temple, and asked how he could help with the repairs to the east wall, which pleased them all. Then he abruptly stood up, dismissed them, and walked out. Simon had to hurry to catch up with him. When they reached the Queen's apartments, Herod dismissed Simon with a wave of his hand, and disappeared inside.

Simon went back to his rooms to see if Sandy was there. She wasn't. He was tired so he lay down and played with his tape recorder. He was careful not to let anyone see it. He knew that they would be so frightened by its 'magic', that he would certainly be killed as a sorcerer. This was why he always carried it everywhere with him. He had just fallen asleep when a slave came to tell him that he was wanted in the King's apartments.

He found the King in a furious rage, which he was trying to control. He snapped at Simon, asked him where he had been, and then didn't listen to the reply. He held in his hand a small sealed scroll.

'Come here, boy, and listen,' he said, putting his hand on Simon's shoulder. 'It seems I can trust no one but you.' He handed Simon the scroll. 'Take this. As soon as it is dark, deliver it to the wise men. You will find them in the High Priest's guest-wing. Then bring them to me through the secret entrance. No one is to know they are here. You understand?'

Simon bowed his head and left. Back in his room he waited for Sandy. When she came in she told him that Herod and the Queen had been having a dreadful quarrel. She had been sent out, but not before she had seen Herod trying to throttle the Queen! She didn't know what it was all about, but she felt that the Queen was trying to persuade Herod not to do something.

'He was in a bad temper afterwards when I saw him,' said Simon. He told her about bringing the wise men secretly to the palace after dark. 'You don't think he's going to kill them do you?'

Sandy said she hoped not, but as he was as mad as a hatter, anything could happen.

'I'll warn them of his temper,' said Simon, 'there's nothing else I can do.'

When it was dark, after making sure no one was in sight, Simon walked out of the side entrance and along to the High Priest's house. He had borrowed a cloak to cover his uniform so that he would not be recognised as a palace servant. He knew exactly where the wise men would be, and managed to run inside the building without being seen. The three men were astonished to read the urgent and secret summons from the King. They knew of his reputation and were rather frightened. They asked Simon if he knew what the King wanted. He told them he didn't know, but they would beware of his temper! They agreed amongst themselves that they had no choice but to go.

Soon they were all following Simon through the secret entrance, (which everyone knew about, but only the King was allowed to use), and into the King's private audience room. Simon presented them to the King at the bottom of the steps, and took up his position, as usual, behind the throne.

The King welcomed them to Jerusalem. He told them that he had heard they were following a star and were looking for the new born Messiah. He said he wanted to help them.

'I have enquired from my priests and scribes where He is to be born, and they are quite sure that it must be in Bethlehem,' he told them. 'That is

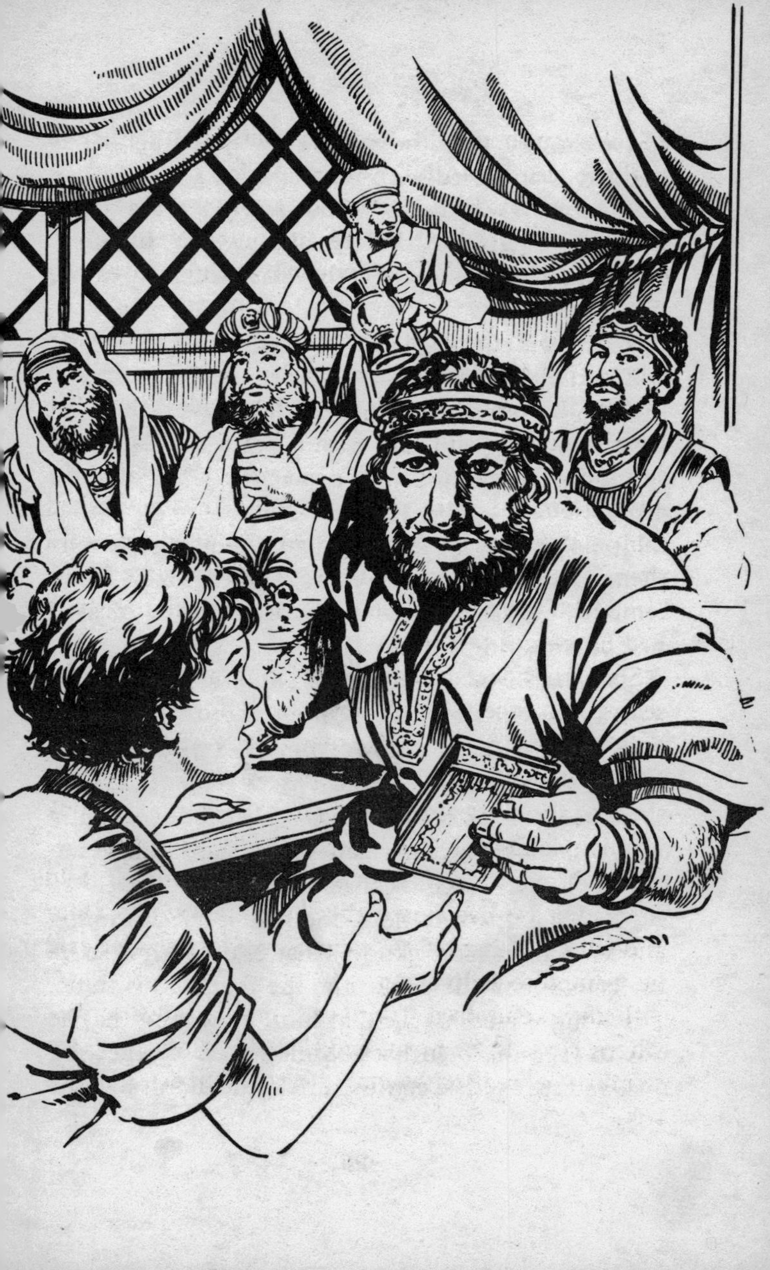

where the star will lead you.' He clapped his hands and slaves appeared with food and wine which they set before the wise men. Herod clearly wanted to put them at their ease, before slipping in his next question. He waited until they had finished eating and drinking.

'When did the star first appear in the sky?' he asked leaning forward so as not to miss the reply.

They discussed this amongst themselves, then the oldest stood up and said with a bow, 'It was over a year ago, Your Majesty. We have travelled far since then.'

Herod smiled at them. He had the information he wanted. This meant that the age of the child could be anything up to about two years. He was pleased with the evening's work. 'You are nearly at the end of your journey,' he said. 'Go to Bethlehem and as soon as you find the babe, send me word where He is so that I may come and worship Him also.'

They thanked him, and, as was the custom, presented him with a gift. It was a small, beautifully carved sandalwood box, almost the same shape and size as Simon's tape recorder.

The King thanked them, and held it out for Simon to take. Simon didn't know what to do with it so he put it in one of the pockets in the folds of his tunic. The King waved his hand at him, indicating that he was to take the men back. Simon wasn't expecting this, and was a little confused. Also he didn't like the look on the King's face. He felt sure he was plotting something. He thought quickly that he had better not take the box with him, so he took it out of his pocket and put it on the side table near the bowl of fruit, all the time hardly taking his eyes off the King, so shocked was he by the look of him.

After wishing the wise men goodnight at the High Priest's house, he made his way back to the palace. The streets were deserted, but the full moon gave the buildings a magical beauty. He took his recorder from his pocket with the thought of playing himself some music quietly. There was no one about so it was quite safe. He had recorded some 'Top of the Pops' songs that night before they left home. It felt rather light in his hand. He stopped and looked at it in horror. It was Herod's box! By mistake he had left the tape recorder on the table! He began to run as he had never run in his life before. All he could think of all the way to the palace was the King picking it up. If he had, and even more if he had played with it and pressed the button, Simon knew that he was as good as dead. He would be killed as a magician or sorcerer!

Chapter Ten

Simon used the secret way in again as it was quicker. He ran across the courtyard, through the great hall, and arrived at the entrance to the private audience room in a state of collapse. Hanging on with both hands to the heavy curtains that hung across the entrance, he peeped through the join in the middle. The throne was empty. Herod had left. On the table he could see the little recorder where he had left it near the bowl of fruit. He was safe!

Sandy found him a few minutes later, still holding onto the curtains, but sitting on the floor, panting heavily, and looking rather pale. He told her what had happened. She went in, and up the steps to the table, took the recorder and brought it back to him.

'You left it switched on to "record",' she said as

she gave it to him. 'I've switched it off, but I expect the battery is finished.'

'I've got news for you,' he smiled at her. 'I didn't tell you, but I carried a spare battery with me.' They laughed and walked back together to their rooms.

The next morning Simon got up early to attend to the King. Sandy had the day off as the Queen had gone to Jericho to visit friends. She decided that she would have a lazy day. First she would bathe, and after dressing go and see old Simeon. Simon told her that someone had seen the cross in the castle, and he was hoping to get it back soon.

'If I get it back today, we could go home tomorrow,' he said. 'What day will it be when we arrive back?'

Sandy thought hard. 'The same night as when we left. That was the night of Christmas Day I think, so we get back for Boxing Day. It seems such a long time ago. Please lend me your tape recorder.'

Simon was about to leave. He took it from his pocket, looked at her, and hesitated.

'*Please!* Simon.'

'All right, but don't let anyone *see* or *hear* it,' he answered her, 'or we shall both be killed as witches or sorcerers or something.' He thought for a moment. 'Can you imagine Herod's face if we played him, "Save Your Kisses For Me"!' They both laughed, so much that tears were streaming from Sandy's eyes. Simon gave her the recorder then with an airy wave of his hand, left for the King's apartments.

She sat up and combed her hair. Then she decided to have some music. Remembering that last night Simon had left the recorder with nothing happening, she reversed the tape some way and then pressed the button to play. She put it on the table and sat back and enjoyed the music which Simon had taped from one of his records. She was just about to switch the volume down, when suddenly the music stopped dead and Herod's voice shouted, 'Come here, you fool!' Then there was nothing. She got such a fright that she was too petrified to move. Then the voice started again from the recorder.

'Go and fetch the scribe. Hurry! Hurry!'

Another long pause. Sandy's eyes were glued to the little tape recorder. Then it started again.

'Write. To my loyal servant, Zedekiah, at Herodium. I am waiting to hear from certain wise men of the whereabouts of a child I wish to have killed. You will be ready with your men to move immediately to Bethlehem. As soon as I hear from the wise men where the child is to be found, I will inform you by special messenger.' Another pause. Sandy held her breath in horror. 'Send it to Herodium first thing tomorrow morning.'

The recorder ran on and on with no more sound until Sandy switched it off. Slowly she realised what had happened. When Simon left the recorder on the table near the throne by mistake, he had left the button in the 'record' position. Herod had waited until Simon was out of the way, and then made his wicked plan. He was going to make sure that no one was going to take his place as King.

She jumped out of bed, washed and dressed quickly, and after hiding the recorder, ran through the palace to the King's apartments. She stopped behind a pillar in the main entrance hall. The King was pacing up and down, surrounded by his ministers. She saw Simon standing on the other side of the hall, watching the King in case he was wanted. She waved frantically trying to attract his attention. He didn't see her. She *had* to tell him of the dreadful danger that threatened Jesus. There was only one thing to do. Making sure she couldn't be seen, she put two fingers in her mouth and let out a piercing whistle. Simon had taught her how to do it at the beginning of the holidays and they had made it their secret signal to each other.

The King and everyone else stopped dead, and looked in her direction. They looked at each other, then round the hall and up at the ceiling. Then, because they couldn't account for the strange noise, they went on with their conversation.

Simon walked round the hall looking for her, hoping the King wouldn't notice his absence. From behind the pillar Sandy signalled him to follow and ran back to their rooms. Simon arrived seconds later.

She made him sit on the bed. 'Just listen to this,' she said, taking the recorder and reversing the tape. She watched her brother's face as Herod began his terrible letter. When it was over, he was too shocked to say anything for a time.

'We've got to warn Mary and Joseph. They *must* get Jesus away somewhere. First we must warn the wise men not to tell Herod where Jesus is. They went to Bethlehem yesterday evening after I took them back to the High Priest's house. They are probably there now.' He sat down in the chair, and held his head in his hands, trying to think what to do. 'If we leave right away, we could be in Bethlehem tonight, but we must move!'

They would remember that journey for the rest of their lives. They ran and walked alternately most of the way. It was dusty, it was hot, it was hell! They carried only a few belongings, which of course included the torch and the tape recorder. After three hours they were in sight of Bethlehem, but Sandy was exhausted. They had to stop and rest.

Lying under a tree, watching the sun sink below the hills, they were able to discuss things together for the first time that day.

'We can't ever go back to the palace after this, that's for sure,' said Simon. 'The King will have another fit when he hears that we have gone. That means I shall never see my cross again.'

Sandy took her ring off her finger and looked at it.

'We can always get out of danger by using the ring to get home,' she said. Simon was looking so despondent that, impulsively, she took his hand and put it on one of his fingers. 'You wear it for a while,' she said, 'But don't lose it, or we shall be in big trouble!'

Simon was very touched. He put it on his finger, being careful not to turn it round. 'Thanks, Sandy,' he said, 'I promise I won't lose it.' He helped her to stand up. 'It will soon be dark, we had better move on. Not far to go now. I only hope that we're in time!'

Everyone they asked in Bethlehem seemed to know where Joseph the carpenter lived, and they were directed to a small house with a carpenter's shop on one side, just outside the town.

It was quite dark by the time they knocked on the door. It was opened by Joseph, whose surprise and pleasure at seeing them again was checked when he saw how tired and travel-stained they were. After taking off their sandals and helping them to wash their feet, he led them inside. He told them that Mary and Jesus were sleeping and asked them to sit down.

They told him everything about Herod's letter, except about the tape recorder, and waited for him to speak.

He seemed to take the news very calmly. 'First, thank you both for coming to warn us,' he said. 'The wise men left early this morning. They knew somehow that Herod was plotting to kill Jesus, so they told me before leaving that they were going home another way.' He poured them a cup of water and handed them some pieces of bread. Then he went on, 'I have had a dream. A dream to tell me to take Jesus and His mother to Egypt. In view of all you have told me, I think we should leave immediately.'

The children agreed, and said that they would wish to go with them on the road south until they were safely on their way, and were able to join a caravan which would give them protection. Joseph thanked them again, and two hours later, after some frantic packing, they all left.

They took two donkeys. The family one for Mary and Jesus, and one that Joseph had bought recently, which carried the household utensils, food, carpenter's tools and blankets. The gifts that the wise men had given Jesus were packed in a special box by Mary and carried by Joseph on his back. Sandy led Mary's donkey, and Simon the other one. The lamb and the chickens had to be left with a kindly neighbour who promised to look after them until Joseph returned. It was a bitterly cold night, and they plodded wearily on, too cold and tired to talk. Then, as dawn began the miracle of a new day, they stopped near a small stream, unloaded the second donkey, and sank wearily to the ground.

They had left Bethlehem only a few miles behind and so they were still in danger. The children collected dry wood for a fire, and after Mary had prepared them a hot drink and some food, and had fed Jesus, they all slept for a few hours. Then off again.

It was on the second night that they found themselves in the greatest danger, and ever afterwards the children were to remember the spider that saved them all.

They had camped for the night in a cave, a little way up the hill from the road. Before the children fell asleep they watched a little spider begin to make a beautiful web across the narrow entrance. He worked so hard and so fast that Sandy said he must be working especially to protect the baby Jesus from the cold night air coming in. When they woke up in the early morning the spider, who must have worked hard all night, had completed his web right across the entrance. What made them all gasp with delight, (and even Jesus gave a smile and a gurgle when He saw it), was that it was sparkling white with hoar frost. Then Sandy remembered the vision she had seen when they were putting tinsel on a Christmas tree at home.

At that moment they heard the sound of galloping horses coming along the road from Bethlehem. It was Herod's soldiers looking for the child! They stopped below on the road to water their horses.

Inside the cave they watched in horror as two men climbed toward them. Some distance away they heard a man shout out something. Then nearer they heard:

'There's nothing round here. Have a look in that cave!'

They held their breath as two men came towards the entrance.

'There's a huge spider's web across the entrance,' said one of them, 'there couldn't be anyone in there. Come on let's go.'

They waited silently while the two soldiers scrambled down to the road and joined their troop. After a long discussion, the leader gave the order to return to Bethlehem.

When they had all left, and the sound of horses hooves had faded in the distance, Joseph gave thanks and they continued their journey. They were still hoping to catch up with a caravan on its way to Egypt. The area they were in was dangerous, as it was often chosen by robbers who attacked small groups of people. Usually they stripped them of everything they had, and then killed them so as not to be recognised afterwards. At midday they came across tracks of recent-looking fires in an encampment where there also had been many camels, so they knew they were not far behind. They would soon be safe with a large caravan that could protect itself.

That evening, as darkness fell, they came to some trees with water nearby and decided to camp for the night. The children had collected sufficient wood for a fire and, because they were tired after their long day's journey, they were resting before cooking an evening meal. Jesus was asleep in Mary's arms.

Suddenly, from out of the darkness five men appeared, armed with rough swords and daggers. One of them held a dagger at Joseph's throat while two of them started to loot the camp. It was useless to resist. The children were too frightened to move. The other two men were about to kill them all when the leader, who had been looking steadily at Jesus as He lay asleep in Mary's arms, shouted, 'Stop!' He ordered the men not to touch anything or harm anyone. Then, again he looked hard at Jesus, kneeling down on one knee in front of Mary, and said softly, 'O blessèd child, if ever there comes a time for having mercy on me, please remember me and forget not this hour.'

The children looked at him, then at each other. It was Dismas! He hadn't seen their faces in the shadows. He looked up and saw them. 'A double cause for not harming anyone!' he cried as he got up and hugged them both. 'You saved me from prison and death. Now what can I do for you?' He led them, one either side of him, away from the camp to where someone was holding his horse. 'We all escaped from the castle, thanks to you,' he said as he mounted.

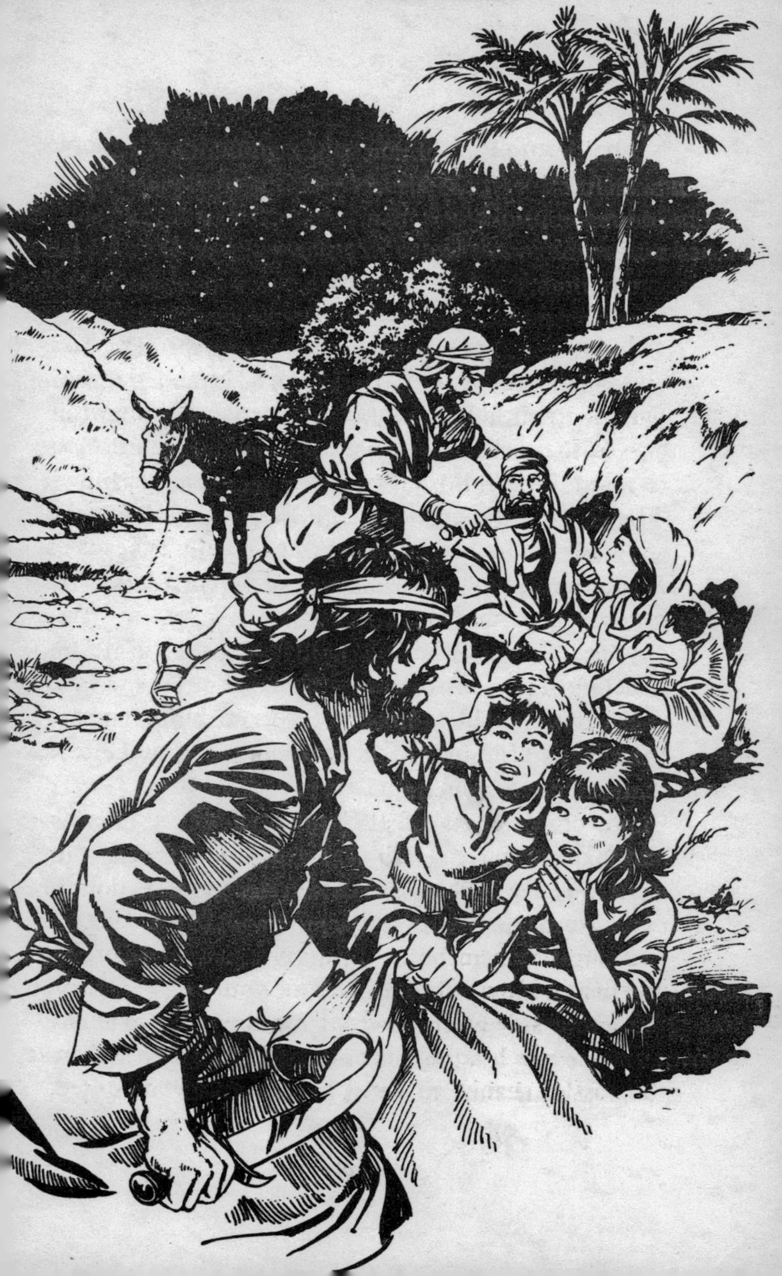

'Now tell me what I can give you in return.'

Sandy said, 'There's nothing I want, thank you, we were glad to help.' She was still frightened of this huge man who was a robber and a thief, but for reasons she couldn't understand, she liked him.

Simon smiled sadly.

'There's only one thing I want,' he said to Dismas, 'and that's my cross. But you can't help with that. I lost it when the Romans were knocking us about in the castle.'

Dismas patted his horse's neck and looked down at Simon. He chuckled in his beard and his eyes twinkled.

'Would it, by any chance, be a *gold* cross?' he asked.

Simon looked up at him in surprise. 'Yes, it is,' he answered.

'With an engraving of a fish on one side?'

'Yes,' said Simon, 'have you seen it?' Now he was really getting excited.

'With the corners a little worn?' continued Dismas with his head on one side, pretending to try hard to remember what it looked like.

'Yes, yes, that's it!'

'With a little hole through which has been threaded a piece of string?'

'*Please*, Dismas!' replied Simon, unable to bear the suspense any longer, 'Please tell me where you saw it. I'd do anything to get it back.'

Dismas put his free hand in the folds of his cloak and suddenly the little cross was hanging in the air, suspended by the string from Dismas' thumb and forefinger.

Dismas smiled at the look of joy he saw on Simon's face. He dropped it gently into his outstretched hands. 'I found it on one of the soldiers whom you tripped down the steps in the castle. He'd cracked his head open so it wasn't much good to him. So I, er,' (here he looked a little guilty), 'I borrowed it from him!'

He gave a great bellow of laughter, dug his heels into the horse's side, waved goodbye to the children and galloped off into the night.

Chapter Eleven

Simon took the ring off his finger and gave it back to Sandy. Then he slipped the cross over his head and hung it round his neck.

'Now you're safe again, whatever happens,' he said to Sandy with a sigh of relief. 'It was good of Dismas to give it back to me, but I do wish that he would stop robbing people. He's sure to be caught one day and the penalty is death by crucifixion.'

They walked back to the camp and found Mary and Joseph preparing a meal of bread and soup. Simon was about to show them his cross and tell them how Dismas had returned it to him, when Sandy put her hand on his arm and stopped him. 'No, don't show them the cross,' she whispered, 'it will upset them.'

After they had eaten they sat round the fire and sang a song (which Joseph said had been written by King David) which began 'The Lord is my Shepherd'. It reminded them how near they were to God always, and how He had protected them on the journey and saved them from the attack by Dismas. Then Joseph gave them his blessing and they settled down to sleep: the baby Jesus in Mary's arms covered by her cloak and a rough blanket, Joseph near the fire with a pile of sticks to keep it going through the night, and the children round their own fire near the donkeys.

The next morning they soon caught up with the caravan which was taking a day's rest before crossing into Egypt. There were some twenty camels and thirty donkeys and nearly fifty men, women and children. They were welcomed by the owner, Ali Khan, who was a rich rug and carpet merchant. He told them that Egypt was only a day's journey to the south and he would be pleased to offer them protection.

The children breathed a sigh of relief. Now they knew that at last the baby must soon be safe. They wandered a little way from the camp and sat down under the shade of a thorn tree.

'Now we can go home,' said Sandy. She thought about home and how much she missed her father and Ding. She thought how wonderful it would be to sleep between sheets again and have apple pie and cream, and real sweets and comfortable clean clothes.

'I wouldn't mind going on to see Egypt,' said Simon, 'but I suppose we should go home.' He stretched out on the warm sand and, propping himself up on an elbow, watched the camels and donkeys being led down to the well to be watered. He took the little recorder from his inside pocket, grinned at Sandy and after reversing it to the beginning, started it off softly.

The music had just begun when they noticed that everyone in the camp was standing and staring back along the road that led north to Bethlehem.

The children stood up. Simon switched his recorder off. They saw in the distance a lone rider on a white horse galloping towards the camp. The horse was clearly very tired as it stumbled several times, but the rider was urging it on with his stick. They ran over to the group of people who were gathered together, waiting to hear the reason for this strange happening. Only rich men were able to afford horses, and no one ever rode in these parts alone.

As he got nearer, the children saw that it was Herod's Chief Steward who had been so kind to them in the Palace. The horse, a mare covered in sweat, halted before them and someone caught the rider as he slipped off and tried to stand. As they laid him on a reed mat, he noticed the children and beckoned them over to him. The people parted as the children approached and knelt down on either side of him. He looked very tired, and he couldn't speak until he had been given some water.

'Herod has had all the male babies up to two years old killed by his soldiers,' he whispered. 'It was dreadful. He wanted to be sure that the new baby king was killed wherever He was.'

He closed his eyes and waited until his strength returned.

'You see, the three wise men returned home without telling Herod where exactly the baby was living. He went into a rage and blamed me because you had both run away. Then he ordered that you both be found and killed as well. I stole a horse from the stables to warn you.'

He motioned for some more water and someone handed Sandy a bowl of water. Gently she raised his head and helped him to drink again.

'In Bethlehem they told me you had left for Egypt. Herod's best horsemen from Herodium arrived before I left. They can only be an hour behind me. You must hurry, the border is only a day away and once across it you will all be safe.'

He closed his eyes. 'I have been riding all night. I must sleep.'

Now the children could hardly hear what he was saying. They bent down closer.

'Take the horse,' he whispered, 'she will carry you both.'

His head fell back and he was fast asleep.

Ali Khan gave orders that the whole caravan was to be ready to move off as soon as possible. Everyone knew what would happen if Herod's soldiers caught up with them. The children helped to put the sleeping steward onto a small two-wheeled donkey cart, then they helped Mary and Joseph to load up the donkeys. Everyone was shouting. The animals were frightened and wouldn't stand still, but at last they were ready to move off. Simon had found the steward's white mare. She had been fed and watered by a servant, and Simon led her back to the tail-end of the caravan where Mary and Jesus were moving off on a donkey with Joseph holding the bridle.

They had hardly moved a few hundred yards along the rough road when someone gave a shout and pointed behind them. In the far distance, three or four miles away, a large cloud of sand and dust moved along the ground. Herod's horsemen. Now there seemed no hope that any of them would reach Egypt alive, although they urged the animals on with shouts and blows, it was clear that there was little or no hope of getting to the border before the horsemen caught up with them.

Sandy was riding the mare next to Mary's donkey, and Simon was walking between them. He thought of giving the mare to Mary so that she could gallop off with Jesus, but he knew that she would not leave Joseph, and the horse would not be able to carry all three. Suddenly he had an idea as he remembered the steward's last words to them.

'Take the horse, she will carry you both.'

'Sandy, I want you to trust me. There's no time to explain. Say goodbye quickly because we're going home!'

He jumped up behind Sandy, put his arms on either side of her, and took the reins. They said goodbye to Mary and Joseph, and little Jesus.

'Thank you for your help,' Joseph said to them both, 'May God go with you.'

Mary raised her hand and smiled.

'Thank you for everything,' she said.

Then Simon did an extraordinary thing. He turned the horse round, and telling Sandy to hold on tight, galloped the horse back along the road towards the approaching horsemen.

Sandy gave a shriek.

'We're going straight for the soldiers!'

'Trust me!' shouted Simon, above the noise of the wind whistling past them and the thudding of the horse's hooves in the sand.

'When we get near them, we'll turn left or right and make them chase us. This will give the caravan time to escape.'

'Thank you!' shouted Sandy back, holding onto the mane with both hands. 'And when they catch us they'll kill us!'

'Sandy,' laughed Simon, 'I'm not stupid you

know. Just before they catch us we'll use the ring to go home!'

Sandy gave one of her special shrieks of delight. She turned her head and smiled at Simon.

'Right!' she shouted, 'Let's give them a good run.'

By now the distance between them and the horsemen galloping towards them was only about a mile. Simon thought that there were about thirty of them. It was nearly time to turn off the road. He prayed that they would follow him.

Sandy listened to him talking quietly to himself, his mouth just behind her left ear.

'We must turn a ninety-degree right angle to the right. That will mean they will be held up by having to round that clump of rocks. Steady . . . steady . . . now!' A gentle pressure on the right rein and a tap with the right heel brought the horse round in a circle. Then she straightened out and Simon let her have her head. It was a ride they were to remember all their lives.

Chapter Twelve

They looked behind them and saw with relief that all the horsemen had turned off the road and were following them, riding as hard as they could, led by a huge man with a black beard. In his right hand he carried a long sword which glistened in the sunlight.

The poor horse that had carried the steward all night was beginning to tire. She was getting slower and slower, but still she gave all her strength to carrying the children to safety.

'We *must* try and delay them a little longer,' Simon said to Sandy, 'and don't use the ring until you feel me grip your left arm. I'll wait until they are within a few yards of us.'

They both looked behind them again. The galloping horses were getting nearer. The man with the sword was waving it in the air. Simon thought how easily he could cut both their heads off. Suddenly the mare stumbled. She could give no more. She simply died on her feet and collapsed onto the sand. The children were thrown clear a little distance apart. All the wind had been knocked out of them. Simon tried to stand to go to Sandy but his left leg had been broken and he gave a shout of pain as he tried to stand.

'Come to me quickly, Sandy. I can't move.'

Sandy was dazed and shocked by the fall and couldn't take in what he was saying. Simon started to crawl towards her, but he was too late. The horsemen were upon them. They were surrounded by horses' legs and shouting men.

Simon was pulled to his feet. He screamed as the bone in his broken leg gave a crunch, but held firmly by his left arm he managed to stand on one leg.

'If only I could get to her,' he thought, 'She will turn the ring round and we shall be safe.' Only five yards of desert between death and home!

The man with the beard had pulled Sandy to her feet and was asking her questions. She seemed to have recovered. She looked at Simon imploring him with her eyes to come to her. Simon was thinking hard. He couldn't go to her, so she must come to him. Suddenly the idea came to him in a flash. Slowly so that no one would notice, he put his right hand inside the folds of his shirt and felt the little tape recorder. He felt for the 'On' button and pressed it. Then with his finger he turned the volume up to 'Full'. Then he withdrew his hand.

The voice of Herod the King blared forth from somewhere inside him, 'Come here, you fool!'

The soldiers all stopped whatever they were doing and stood, transfixed by fear.

Simon shouted to Sandy to come to him but she was still being held by her arms. Then came the voice again, 'Go and fetch the scribe. Hurry! Hurry!'

Now the soldiers were really frightened. They knew Herod's voice only too well. This was magic!

The man holding Sandy let go of her for an instant, his mouth open in amazement at what he heard. She lunged forward and ran over to Simon who reached out and held her arm with his one free hand. Sandy turned the ring round and round and round.

It was the smoothest trip they had ever made. They both woke up in their own beds with the winter sun streaming through the windows.

Sandy lay for a moment with her eyes open. She thought how nearly their plan had gone wrong because they were going to use the ring while they were still on the horse. She thought how clever Simon had been to use his recorder. She thought about Mary and Joseph and Jesus, and hoped that they were safe in Egypt. She thought how lovely it was to be home again in her own bed.

Simon stretched himself. Then he remembered his leg. He couldn't feel any pain. He sat up and felt it with both his hands right the way down from top to toe over his pyjamas. It was all healed. He felt for his cross round his neck. It was still there. On the table next to his bed lay the little recorder that had saved them.

Sandy came through and sat on his bed. She was relieved to find that his leg was completely healed.

'You know, Simon, we nearly didn't get home,' she said, thinking how close it had been, 'but what an adventure!'

Simon agreed. He was already looking forward to another adventure. 'Next time we use the ring we may find ourselves anywhere.'

'Yes,' said Sandy, 'but I'm sure that we were meant to find the cross and the ring so that we could help somebody. Anyhow, let's go on keeping it as a secret. If we told people, even Dad, it might not work again.'

Just then the door opened and their father came into the room. Sandy rushed over, threw herself into his arms and smothered him in kisses. Simon got out of bed and joined them.

'This is all very well,' their father laughed, 'but anyone would think that you'd just returned from a distant land!'

The children looked at each other, and then began to laugh so much that tears streamed from their eyes.

When Dad saw that they were going on and on he thought it was very odd as he didn't think he had said anything funny. He looked at his watch.

'I'm late for surgery again,' he said and hurried downstairs.

Ding called up that breakfast was ready, and what were they doing?

The children by now had exhausted their laughter.

'It's just as if nothing had happened,' said Simon to Sandy 'They did get to Egypt safely, didn't they?'

Sandy hurried back to her room and returned with her Bible.

'Of course they did,' she replied. She opened it and found the place.

'Here it is.'

'Matthew, Chapter two, Verse thirteen,' she read out.

'... an angel of the Lord appeared to Joseph in a dream, and said to him, 'Rise up, take the child and his mother and escape with them to Egypt, and stay there until I tell you; for Herod is going to search for the child to do away with him.' So Joseph rose from sleep, and taking mother and child by night he went away with them to Egypt, and there he stayed till Herod's death.'